Albert Bigelow Paine, William Allen White

Rhymes by two Friends

Albert Bigelow Paine, William Allen White

Rhymes by two Friends

ISBN/EAN: 9783743305007

Manufactured in Europe, USA, Canada, Australia, Japa

Cover: Foto ©Andreas Hilbeck / pixelio.de

Manufactured and distributed by brebook publishing software
(www.brebook.com)

Albert Bigelow Paine, William Allen White

Rhymes by two Friends

INTRODUCTION.

A NUMBER of the poems in this collection have been printed and praised by newspapers and magazines East, West, North, South. So many people have shown an interest in them that the authors are encouraged to hope that selections of their work between book-covers will afford some degree of satisfaction to the public. They have not re-strung the lute of Mr. Apollo, or interrupted the corn-planting of Mrs. Ceres; they have in no way offended the Kansans' ideas of poesy—for the best poetry made in Kansas is not that of the Study. It does not smell of the midnight oil. There is no Greek or Latin flavor to it. Time-worn Mythological figures have no place in its construction. Even songs of Ruins, of Moonlight, of Babbling Brooks have given way to living fancies. One sees and feels all that is here written.

The "Rhymes of Two Friends" recall memories we love—the sound of a voice, the smile of a face, the touch of a hand. They appeal to the heart and soften the hard places in the struggle for life. Surrendering to their charms one becomes a Boy Innocent, a Young Man Eloquent. an Old Man Reminiscent. We shall be the better for reading these Rhymes again and again.

EWING HERBERT.

HIAWATHA, KANS., *Aug. 15, 1893.*

CONTENTS.

Rhymes.

THE NUMBER OF BOOKS IN THIS
EDITION IS LIMITED TO FIVE HUNDRED
OF WHICH THIS IS

No. 332.

Acknowledgements are due Messrs. Harper & Bros., editors of Ladies' Home Journal, Worthington's Magazine, Truth, Kansas City Star and others for reprint here of a number of these rhymes.

THE ORGANIST.

SHE was born in cultured Boston, in
    that fair and famous town,
And her father was a financier of
    venture and renown ;
She acquired an education of the old New Eng-
    land kind,
Hoarding stores of classic wisdom in a compre-
    hensive mind ;
But her music, Oh, her music, 'twas her soul's
    transcendent glory !
And she finished with a flourish in the big con-
    servatory ;
Finished with a theme from Mozart—'mid the
    plaudits of the throng
That arose and filled her being like a symphony
    of song.

Ah, these earthly joys are transient and depart
    on noiseless wings,
And our wealth's the most uncertain of all insub-
    stantial things :
Thus one morning when the market stumbled
    down a steep incline
All the father's fortune crumbled in a Colorado
    mine ;
And although he tried to rally on a little deal in
    wheat,   .
Still the luck kept hard against him till it cleaned
    him out complete.

Gone their fortune, friends and fireside—gone
    the grand piano, too--
They must seek some humble shelter and begin
    the world anew ;

    And the old man, full of sorrow, said
        he could'nt bear to stay
    In the place that saw his ruin, so
        they sadly crept away ;
    But they left behind the mother,
        she the happiest of all,—
    She had died amid their plenty just
        a year before the fall.

And they came out to the prairies and they humbly settled down
On a little stony forty 'bout a mile or so from town ;
Where the father, half discouraged, struggled hard to make a stand,
But they only grew the poorer on that stony bit of land ;
While the daughter, spirit-broken, plodding hopelessly along,
Half forgot her classic learning and the symphony of song ;
Half forgot her Latin verses, learning how to cook and scrub ;
Half for-

got the themes of Mozart in the music of the tub.

Only, now and then at evening, when the sun was going down,
And the green upon the meadow faded softly into brown,

She would slip across the upland to a lonely
    clump of birch
Where she knew there was an organ in a little
    country church.

There amid the shades of evening she would sit
    alone and play,
While her soul from earthly travail seemed to
    lift and soar away.
'Twas the single hour of triumph in the weary
    round she trod ;
'Twas the resonant outpouring of the spirit to
    its God.

I I

By and by the old man tottered and was helpless
      in his chair ;

And the heart-sick daughter married in a sort of
      wild despair ;

Took a man who owned a section and a half of
      fertile clay,

And for this she swore to love him, and to honor,
      and obey ;

Took a man whose education was confined to
      cows and corn ;

Took a man whose sweetest music was the rasp-
      ing dinner horn ;

Who on Sunday sang Old Hundred in an ancient
      nasal way,

Knowing less of time than turnips—less of har-
      mony than hay.

One more night she crossed the upland and pour-
      ed out her heart to God,

Then forever barred its portals and was mated
      with a clod.

But the neighbors called him "dea-
      con," for he led the hymn
      and prayer,

And on Sunday walked to "meetin'" with
    a self-complacent air ;
And the woman walked beside him, humbly
    heeding his command,
He the owner of a section and a half of fer-
    tile land ;
And she hearkened to the preacher, cringing at
    his nasal twang,
And she played the little organ when the
    congregation sang.
But she came no more at evening to pour
    out her soul alone ;
She had bartered soul for substance, and
        her heart was turned to stone.

Thus the years went creeping onward, and
      the babies came along,
Each with voice attuned to mingle in a
    swelling choric song ;
While the mother, bowed and broken,
    toiling early, toiling late,
Long ago has ceased from troubling and resigned
    herself to fate ;
Long ago has she forgotten all her
    precious classic lore

And the magic themes of Mozart wake her spirit
    never more ;
Long ago has ceased from sighing at the father's
    empty chair
And the old man, 'neath the clover, slumbers on
    and does not care.

Still she hearkens to the deacon heeding all he
    has to say ;
Still performs her wifely duties in an uncom-
    plaining way ;
Still each Sunday plays the organ, down amid the
    clump of birch,
For the singing of Old Hundred in that little
    country church.

A DREAM OF THE SEA.

FARMER lad in his prairie home
        Lay dreaming of the sea !
    He ne'er had seen it, but well he knew
Its pictured image and heavenly hue ;
And he dreamed he swept o'er its waters blue,
        With the winds a-blowing free,
        With the winds so fresh and free.

He woke ! and he said "The day will come
        When that shall be truth to me ;"
But as years swept by him he always found
That his feet were clogged and his hands were
    bound,
Till at last he lay in a narrow mound,
        Afar from the sobbing sea,
        The sorrowing, sobbing sea.

Oh, many there are on the plains to-night,
      That dream of a voyage to be;
And have said in their souls "The day will come
When my bark shall sweep through the drifts
    of foam !"
But their eyes grow dim and their lips grow dumb,
      Afar from the tossing sea,
      The turbulent, tossing sea.

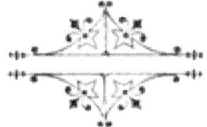

FIRST BRIGHT DAYS.

When the skies are getting bluer and the fields
    are getting green,
When the bud upon the maple is beginning to be
    seen—
Where the willows sweep the water there's a flash
    of silver light,
For the bud is on the maple and the fish begin
    to bite.

Then the world is getting ready for the blossom
    of the spring ;
The sun is creeping northward and the wild duck
    following,
And every day is clipping off a piece from every
    night,

When the bud is on the maple and the fish begin
    to bite.

Oh, days when first the sun breaks through and
    warms the heart to peace !
Oh, days when men grow young again and half
    their troubles cease !
Oh, days when every germ of hope is pushing to
    the light,
And the bud is on the maple and the fish begin
    to bite !

THE LIVES OF MEN.

'Tis strange about the lives of men ;
They live, and love, and die, and then,
What then ?   Ah, don't I wish I knew !
But really cannot tell, can you ?

THE GATES AJAR.

EVENING.

I HAVE seen a Kansas sunset like a vision in a
    dream,
When a halo was about me, and a glory on the
    stream ;
When the birds had ceased their music and the
    summer day was done ;
And prismatic exhalations came adrifting from
    the sun ;
And those gold and purple vapors, and the holy
    stillness there,
Lay upon the peaceful valley like a silent, eve-
    ning prayer ;
And I've gazed upon that atmospheric splendor
    of the west
Till it seemed to me a gateway to the regions of
    the blest.

MORNING.

I HAVE seen a Kansas sunrise like the waking of
    a dream,
When every dewy blade of grass caught up the
    golden gleam ;
When every bird renewed the song it sang the
    night before,
And all· the silent, slumbering world returned to
    life once more ;
When every burst of radiance called up a throng
    of life,
And all the living, waking world with melody
    was rife.
And, as the flood of light and song came floating
    down the plain,
It seemed to me those golden gates were open
    wide again.

MIS' SMITH.

ALL day she hurried to get through
The same as lots of wimmin do ;
Sometimes at night her husban' said,
" Ma, ain't you goin' to come to bed ?"
And then she'd kinder give a hitch,
And pause half-way between a stitch,
And sorter sigh, and say that she
Was ready as she'd ever be,
     She reckoned.

And so the years went one by one,
An' somehow she was never done ;
An' when the angel said, as how
" Mis' Smith, its time you rested now,"
She sorter raised her eyes to look
A second, as a stitch she took ;
" All right, I'm comin' now," says she,
" I'm ready as I'll ever be,
     I reckon."

SOMETIMES.

Sometimes I have dreams of a far-off time
  When the busy world shall a moment cease
Its headlong rush, for some bit of rhyme,
Some newly awakened chord, or chime,
That I may touch in that far-off time
  While groping among the keys.

Sometimes I think that I yet may sing
  A song that never was sung before ;
That I yet may touch some quivering string
Till its slumbering soul shall awake and fling
A song into mine, that I shall sing
  And men will echo forevermore.

THE ISLAND OF LITERATURE.

He who seeks immortal fame—
Seeks to mummify his name
In the isle of literature,
Disappointment must endure
    And abide :
Very hard that isle to enter—
Harder still to reach the center
    Gainst the tide.

From that magic isle of dreams
There are sundry crystal streams
Flowing outward to the sea—
Whence a route, it seems to me,
    Might be had :
But the dragons guarding each,
And the quick-sands of the beach,
    Make it bad.

Budding genius dreams a dream
Of that island, and a stream
Flowing fast and flowing free,
From the center to the sea :
     And he sails,
Thinking he will sail right in—
Thinking he is sure to win,
     But he fails.

Then he skims around the edges,
In the marshes and the sedges ;
But he finds no entrance fair
To that island lying there
     All so calm ;
Still he watches and he waits,
Like a beggar at the gates, .
     For an alm.'

But the days are bleak and dismal,
And the nights appear abysmal :
So, with unrequited yearning,
Sadly, sorrowfully turning,
     Off he goes :
While the tear-drops gently trickle,
Till they form a big icicle
     On his nose.

Some day he may come again—
Some far distant day, and then,
When the best of life is gone,
And the night comes creeping on,
              He may find,
In the island of his dream,
That fair and undiscovered stream
                Left behind.

THE WAKING.

Oh, love of life's morn, when the fresh dew of
      truth
And innocence lies on the tendrils of youth!

As fair as a snowflake untarnished by earth,
As pure as a babe on the day of its birth.

As fair as a lily just burst into bloom,
As sweet as a breath of that lily's perfume.

Bright star of the dawn! Thou forever shalt be
The rarest of all my lost jewels, to me.

THE FISHERMAN.

He left us one evening in late July,
  When the sun was sinking to rest,
He stepped on board as he said "Good-by!"
  And his boat sailed down to the west.

And we watched it slowly go out of sight,
  Where the red was beginning to burn,
And somehow we felt in our hearts that night
  That his boat would never return.

But no one spoke of the half-formed dread
  That lay in each troubled breast;
And we watched each day till the sky burned red
  For the boat that sailed down to the west.

Day after day we paced the sand,
  Still watching; but all in vain;
And I think he sailed to a better land,
  For he never came back again.

THE WAVE AND THE STAR.

FAR on the ocean a billow was born,
A waif of the wind and the sea.
A star up in heaven shone brightly
at morn,
A spark of eternity.

And the beautiful star loved the wave, from afar,
And paled in its mute despair ;
But the wave on its bosom caught up.the star,
And died as it held it there.

THE DANCING BEAR.

Oh, it's fiddle-de-dum and fiddle-de-dee,
The dancing bear ran away with me ;
For the organ grinder he came to town
With a jolly old bear in a coat of brown,
And the funny old chap joined hands with me,
While I cut a caper and so did he.
Then 'twas fiddle-de-dum and fiddle-de-dee,
I looked at him, and he winked at me,
And I whispered a word in his shaggy ear,
And I said, "I will go with you, my dear."

Then the dancing bear he smiled and said,
Well, he didn't say much, but he nodded his head,
As the organ-grinder began to play,
"Over the hills and far away."
With a fiddle-de-dum and a fiddle-de-dee ;

Oh, I looked at him and he winked at me,
And my heart was light and the day was fair,
And away I went with the dancing bear.

Oh, it's fiddle-de-dum and fiddle-de-dee,
The dancing bear came back with me ;
For the sugar-plum trees were stripped and bare,
And we couldn't find cookies anywhere.
And the solemn old fellow he sighed and said,
Well, he didn't say much, but he shook his head,
While I *looked* at him and he *blinked* at me
Till I shed a tear and so did he ;
And both of us thought of our supper that lay
Over the hills and far away.
Then the dancing bear he took my hand,
And we hurried away through the twilight land ;
And 'twas fiddle-de-dum and fiddle-de-dee
When the dancing bear came back with me.

MY THREE FRIENDS.

On the sunlit island of Long-ago—
  In the valley of Used-to-be,
There were three good friends that I used to know
  Who have wandered away from me.

One was buried when life was young—
  His grave is far from me ;
And one I lost by a slandering tongue,
  And one crossed over the sea.

And now as I sit in my room alone,
  They live in my memory ;
And I wonder if any that I have known
  Do ever remember me.

But one passed over the river of death,
  And one crossed over the sea,
And one I lost by a venemous breath—
  And all have forgotten me.

CHRYSANTHEMUM.

Across a waste of moorland, bleak and bare,
　　A lonely bird is flying, calling low—
　　The last of all the feathered host to go,
And loth to leave still lingers, calling, there.
Within my silent garden-passes, where
　　The flowers are withered that in summer blow,
　　I walk with murmuring ghosts, that to and fro
Sway gently in the chill November air ;

When, lo ! I mark a little way apart
　　The sovereign glory of this waning year
　　That now, alone, unheralded hath come,
In gorgeous robes—alas, my fickle heart
　　Forgets the dead, and laughs that she is here,
　　The royal queen of fall, Chrysanthemum.

RESURGAM.

THE year is waning fast, the biting wind
    Is prating through the branches brown and
        sere ;
    Complaining echos voice that fall is here,
And drowsy summer dreaming far behind.
There's death on every hand, and yet I find
    A mournful pomp along these darkened ways,
    So prodigal of bloom in summer days,
When vine and flower in glory intertwined.

Dear wife, along these charnel paths we pass,
    Two silent mourners for the dying year ;
Draw close thy cloak, the wind is chill ; Alas,
    How fast the winter comes ; how reft of cheer
Will be those lagging days ; and yet we know
Our flowers will only sleep, beneath the snow.

THE METHOD IN IT.

WE were playin' a quiet game of draw,
   Muggins an' me an' Looney Ben ;
Queerest old chap you ever saw ;
   (Accident once, an' fits since then.)

Straight enough, though, when his head was right,
   But skeery, you bet, when his spells come on ;
Though things were runnin' on smooth that night,
   As the hands were dealt and the cards were
      drawn.

Lucky old Muggins had won a lot ;
   I was easy—the loss was Ben's.
Mug' had jest opened a big jack-pot,
   And I had filled on a pair of tens.

When all of a sudden Ben giv' a yell
   That lifted our hair and raised the sweat ;
Then just what happened I couldn't tell,
   Fer Ben had a fit, an' we left, you bet !

Deserted like cowards, an' left poor Ben—
   Flew through the window an' took the sash—
I reckon Ben smiled for a 'minit', an' then
   Walked out through the door an' took the cash.

TRIOLET.

A pale, little flaxen tress
   Tied up with a bit of thread ;
Not much to admire, I guess,
Such a pale, little flaxen tress,
Yet I kiss it, and bless, and caress,
   For 'twas clipped from my baby's head,
This pale, little flaxen tress
   Tied up with a bit of thread.

THE BOATSWAIN'S STORY.

"Can I swim? Oh, yes, and I swam right well
　One night down here on this southern coast,
When the wind and the sea were a raging hell,
　And the good ship Mary Lee was lost.

" I was on board that luckless ship—
　I, and about one hundred more.
She had just come in from a three years' trip
　To go down that night within sight of shore.

"We had beaten about with the wind all day,
　Though the most of us knew 'twas a useless
　　　fight ;
And at last, when our rudder was swept away,
　It carried hope with it and sank from sight.

"And we knew that the end was drawing nigh,
　And we felt that the moment was close at hand,
When we'd float away in the sea to die,
　To be cast at morn on the yellow sand.

"Some were in tears and some in prayer,
  And some were singing an old-time psalm ;
And a few of the faces that I saw there
  Were filled with a look of a peaceful calm.

"The captain's daughter—a fair young thing
  Of sixteen summers—shed never a tear ;
But I saw her lips press the golden ring
  On her fair left hand as the end drew near.

"And the strongest men were giving way,
  With curses and prayers in the selfsame breath ;
While the frailest forms that were there that day
  Were calm and brave in the face of death.

"And I've often noticed in times like that,
  That the weak are strong and the strong are
      weak ;
And I think to my death I shall never forget
  The look that night on the strong man's cheek.

"They were first to take to the boats when
      launched,
  And were swamped and lost in the first big sea.
I saw them a moment with faces blanched,
  And then they drifted away from me.

" At last we struck, as we knew we must,
   And we knew it was death when we felt the
     shock.
' *Now each to their God and their strength must*
     trust !'
   The captain cried, '*She is on a rock !'*

" And a moment more I was in the sea,
   Fighting my way through the boiling brine.
I thought that no one was near to me,
   When all of a sudden a hand clasped mine.

" A small, slim hand, and I felt its clasp,
   And knew that its owner was not yet dead.
I took it in mine with a firmer grasp ;
   'We will live or die together,' I said.

" Gods ! how I fought that night with the sea !
   But gaining the battle inch by inch ;
I thought each wave that swept over me
   Must carry me down, but I did not flinch.

" And I held on tight to that little hand,
   That now lay passive and still in mine,
Till at last, thank God, I could touch the sand,
   And drew up my charge from the seething brine.

" I drew it up high on the shelving beach,
   But I could not speak for the breakers' roar.
I staggered up out of the water's reach,
   Then my brain grew numb and I knew no more.

"When life returned it was broad, bright day,
   And the sun was shining above my head.
Close at my side my companion lay.
   'Twas the captain's daughter, and she was
     dead !"

LINES IN A DICTIONARY.

A FEAST of words collected here doth lie,
A wondrous feast of twenty-six rare courses ;
A modest taste of each is all that I
May hope to take, yet Nature's ardent forces,
With every morsel, hungrier than before,
Unsatisfied call lustily for more.

AT GALVESTON.

A LONG, low stretch of sandy beach,
　　Where foamy waves that hurry in,
　　Keep up a never ceasing din ;
And water far as eye can reach.

White sailboats that go flitting by,
　　And white winged sea-gulls, whose frail forms
　　Brave fearlessly the fiercest storms,
Go circling through the summer sky ;

Where fleecy clouds like drifts of snow
　' Float softly on a sea of blue,
　　Whose tender color, melting through,
Lends lustre to the sea below.

Such is the restful vision here
　　By this fair city in the sea,
　　On this low isle that seems to me
Must one day melt and disappear.

IN LOUISIANA.

THE long, gray moss that softly swings
   In solemn grandeur from the trees,
   Like mournful funeral draperies—
A brown-winged bird that never sings.

A shallow, stagnant, inland sea,
   Where rank swamp grasses wave, and where
   A deadliness lurks in the air—
A sere leaf falling silently.

The death-like calm on every hand,
   That one might deem it sin to break,
   So pure, so perfect—these things make
The mournful beauty of this land.

LIFE.

"A LETTER," he gayly said,
  And he handed it to his wife.
It told her, that lying dead,
  Was a friend of her early life.

A ring at the entry door
  Calls for an explanation ;
He returns to his wife once more
  With a wedding invitation.

A call at the telephone,
  And a voice says, "Give me joy,"
And continues in blissful tone,
  "My Mary has got a boy."

EPILOGUE.

And so life scampers past,
  I wonder for which 'tis worst,
The one that marries—or breathes its last,
  Or the one that breathes its first.

A FATAL REFORM.

Sammy Wilkins was a pilot on a lower river
    steamer,
When his flues was charged with lightnin', was a
    howlin' ringtail screamer.
Fond of fair and frail companions—giv'n to
    dealin' from the bottom,
An' he kep a soakin' pizen 'till eventually he
    got 'em.

Well, he went to hear the preacher, an' resolved
    to give up drinkin',
Likewise wimmen, cards, and cussin'—it had
    sorter set him thinkin',
That same night he sailed to glory in a heap of
    wild confusion
Sammy's bark had gone to pieces on the rock of
    resolution.

ON THE GREENBRIAR.

"When the gay little calendar spells July,"
   And the sun is directly overhead—
When quivering motes in the sunbeams fly,
   And your collar is limp and your face is red—

When your blood and your brains are all astew,
   And you're trying to cool them with ices and
      things,
Till at last you hardly know what to do,
   But rush away to the coast and springs,

Then come with me and I'll show you a spot
   Where the mountains are high and the woods
      are dim ;
Where peace is found, and man is not,
   Where all day long by the river's brim

We will lie and dream or drift away
  In a gay little boat with painted oars ;
Watching the clouds, or the trout at play,
  Or the shadows along the shores.

Or the mountains clad in their ranks of pine,
  Away up there a mile and a half
Above the battle and skirmish line,
  While the thought of the heat just makes us
    laugh.

Oh, friends, we are always drifting away
  In a painted boat on memory's stream ;
And the twilight shadows grow long and gray,
  As we lie and drift, as we drift and dream.

Oh, friend, that river is broad and fair,
  And the shadows are soft and the shores are
    dim ;
And the sunlight is flecking the ripples there,
  And the lilies are white along the brim.

But, friend, there are graves along the shore
  Of that river so broad and fair,
And we softly pass them with muffled oar
  For the hopes of our youth lie buried there.

Pshaw ! What am I saying ? We'll start to-day
  For a month in the mountains to rest and
    dream.
Forgive me, old friend, for drifting away
  A moment or two on memory's stream.

THE NORTH SIDE.

Long years ago, one bitter night,
  A storm broke on the fold ;
It touched my breast with its chilling blight
  And left it seared and cold.

Some mellow days the sun comes out
  And sooths the old time smart ;
But patches of snow still cling about
  The north side of my heart.

THE PLANET MARS.

TOGETHER we sat in the summer night,
  (An August night with a wealth of stars)
And we marked where it gleamed so redly bright,
    The Planet Mars.

We spoke of the cruel wrongs of earth,
  Of the host of evils that greed unbars;
And then we spoke of another birth
    In the Planet Mars.

And we wondered if each would know the name
  Of the other, up there, amid the stars,
And we said we hoped they would be the same
    In the Planet Mars.

And so we talked through the summer night,
  Of life and of love amid the stars;
And how our wrongs would be all made right
    In the Planet Mars.

WRITIN' JIM.

HE was what you call a poet, a writin' sort o'
    chap,
Created so by natur' an' a-nussled in her lap.
He was diff'runt from us fellers an' I've heard
    his folks complain,
As Jim's whole make-up, somehow, run abnormal-
    ly to brain.

Not much of ejjication, leastways the printed
    kind ;
But a boy with more of larnin' it was mighty
    hard to find.
He knew most every language that the birds and
    flowers could speak,
But he didn't know no Latin an' he didn't know
    no Greek.

Well, after while, he sorter got ter writin' for the
    press,
An' he found it tough percedin' with them editors
    I guess ;
Fer his spellen' was unsartin' an' his writin'
    kinder queer,
An' them high-flung Eastern fellers they perused
    it with a sneer,
An' his path was mighty thorny an' the win' was
    bleak an' strong,
But he kep' a-cuttin' briars an' mowin' right
    along.

Till, by an' bye, them fellers, they begun to find
    him out,
An' to view their past decisions with a grain er
    two of doubt ;
An' to wonder if their jedgments, they had thought
    so mighty keen,
Hadn't missed, beneath the rough, "a gem of
    purest ray serene."

So they wrote to Jim an' told him that he'd bet-
    ter come to town,—
That they'd like to get acquainted—an' Jim he

hustled down ;

An' now, there in the city, they are makin' heaps
    of him,

An' we up here air mighty proud, to-day, of
    writin' Jim.

AN OASIS.

WHENE'ER I strive in vain to weep
  O'er blighted hopes, or vanished years,
Ah, then, what would I give to steep
  My soul in tears.

For though such tears would flow from me
  As bitter as the springs of Marah,
A sweet oasis it would be
  In life's Sahara.

PEACE.

They have buried me here beneath the sod,
  And heaped a grave up over my head.
The preacher commended my soul to God,
  And they said that I was dead.

They did not know that lying so still
  I could hear all the better the words they said—
They did not know that I felt a thrill
  Of pleasure at knowing that I was dead!

For resting so peacefully here I know
  That the struggle is over and I am free;
And I need not care now for the debts that I owe
  Or the debts that are owing to me.

And a sense of rest has entered my breast
　　That to me is sweet and new;
For the final strife that ended my life
　　Has ended its trials, too.

Truly, the bed they made me is small,
　　But I find it amply wide;
For I never have tossed about at all
　　Since the blessed day I died.

Sweetly, so sweetly I rest and dream
　　With all the old aching gone out of my head.
How strange it is that it used to seem
　　Sad to hear that a friend was dead.

For a wonderful rest has entered my breast,
　　That is perfect and sweet and new;
And the final strife that ended my life
　　Has lifted its burdens, too.

THE SWALLOW AND THE SOUL.

(From the Anglo Saxon.)

As THE swallow that darts through the room of
    light
  From the winter without to the warmth within,
And straight on through, out into the night,
   From the warmth and the glow to the gloom
    again.

So the soul flits in at the door of birth,
  To bask for a moment in life's sweet bloom ;
Speeds, like an arrow, across the earth,
  Then out once more to the night and gloom.

DEPOT.

The girl in sunny Kansas born,
  Whose charms our hearts shall keep, O,
Surveys all foreign airs with scorn
  And says it is "the depo."

The Boston girl, in wonder mild
  That any one should say so,
Reproves the blooming prairie child,
  And murmurs "'tis the daypo."

Chicago's jaunty little miss,
  With accent on the "O"
And lips we vainly long to kiss,
  Pronounces it "de-*po*."

While Baltimore's enchanting girl,
  With dainty grace and step, O,
Gives her bewitching lip a curl
  And sweetly says "the deppo."

Oh, unaffected Kansas born
  Our hearts you're sure to keep, O,
Because all foreign airs you scorn,
  And stick to saying "depo."

KANSAS, THEN AND NOW.

DRENCHED with impetuous martyr blood she
      stands,
A nation's pride—the weeping cynosure
Of all the world.   Deflowered by ruthless hands,
Defamed, dishonored, reft of all that's pure,
To rise a spotless monument, at last,
For all the future and to all the past.

O'ER TURF AND CLOD.

A SUMMER morn in Tennessee
  Was dawning calm and still,
As a gallant horseman rapidly
  Rode down the Jackson hill.
'Twas Captain Gray, and in his breast
  The colonel's order lay,
To ride roughshod o'er turf and clod
  To meet the foe that day.

And now he swiftly spurs along
  Upon his bright bay steed,
And all the while with every mile
  He urges greater speed.
With early dawn the message came
  That sped him on his way,
O'er turf and clod to ride roughshod
  To fight the foe to-day.

Yet, faster, faster over field
   And through the wood he flies,
The early farmer, in alarm,
   Beholds with wond'ring eyes.
Some call to him, but all in vain,
   He will not stop or stay—
Who rides roughshod o'er turf and clod
   To meet the foe to-day.

A streamlet sparkles in his path,
   He pauses on the brink
To give his panting charger breath,
   And let the creature drink.
A moment, then away again,
   Impatient of delay—
O'er turf and clod he flies roughshod
   To fight the foe to-day.

A little hamlet lies before,
   He sweeps through like the wind.
The men turn out and wave, and shout,
   As fast they fall behind ;
While on and on the two have gone,
   The captain and his bay,
O'er turf and clod they fly roughshod
   To meet the foe to-day.

The moments fly, the hours speed by,
　　But never rest takes he ;
The battlefield will soon be nigh.
　　And after victory
On nature's breast the two can rest,
　　God help you, Captain Gray,
To ride roughshod o'er turf and clod
　　To victory to-day.

And now the roll of musketry
　　Comes to him from afar ;
The cannon's boom, the rattling drum,
　　And all the sounds of war—
While faster, faster spurs he on
　　To join the glorious fray ;
O'er turf and clod he flies roughshod
　　To reach the field to-day.

The race is finished—in the fight
　　The death-shots thickly fly,
And brave men fall on left and right,
　　Who conquer but to die.
The victory near, he knows no fear,
　　And revels in the fray—
Who rode roughshod o'er turf and clod
　　To reach the field to-day.

*   *   *   *   *   *   *   *

The battle raged the livelong day,
　At night the foe had fled ;
But lo ! the captain and his bay
　Were lying with the dead.
The tale is told by comrades old,
　And I have heard them say
How, o'er turf and clod to the throne of God,
　The captain rode that day.

WHEN THE SUNFLOWERS BLOOM.

'VE bin off on a journey, I jes' got home to-
    day;
I traveled east an' north, an' south, an'
    every other way;
I've seen a heap o' country, an' cities on the
    boom,
But I want to be in Kansas when the
            Sun-
                Flowers
                    Bloom.

Oh, it's nice among the mount'ns, but I sorter
      felt shet in ;
'Twould be nice upon the seashore ef it wasn't
      fer the din ;
While the prairies air so quiet, an' there's always
      lots o' room ;
Oh, it's nicer still in Kansas when the
                  Sun-
                      Flowers
                          Bloom.

You may talk about yer lilies, yer vi'lets and yer
      roses,
Yer asters, an' yer jassymins an' all the other
      posies ;
I'll allow they all air beauties an' full er sweet
      perfume,
But there's none of 'em a patchin' to the
                  Sun-
                      Flower's
                          Bloom.

When all the sky above is jest ez blue ez blue
  can be,
An' the prairies air a-wavin' like a yallar driftin' sea,
Oh, 'tis here my soul goes sailin' an' my heart is
  on the boom ;
In the golden fields of Kansas when the
     Sun-
      Flowers
       Bloom.

STRAYED.

I WONDER, sometimes, as I sit alone,
  When the cares of the busy day are over,
And the books are closed, and the clerks are gone,
  What has become of that careless rover

That I knew so well some years ago
  As a devil-may-care, wild sort of a fellow,
With a face like mine, only younger you know,
  Not quite so wrinkled, nor half so yellow.

He vanished one glorious day in June,
  The happiest day in all my life; ˜
We never missed him till he was gone,
  And a woman stood by that I called "my wife."

And I soon forgot I had ever known
  Such a devil-may-care, wild sort of a rover,
Save now and then as I sit alone
  When the cares of the busy day are over.

Then, sometimes, I wonder where he can be,
　　For we never have seen him about since then,
But he looked altogether so much like me
　　That I'm glad he never came back again.

THE TOUCH OF ART.

SOMETIMES the day is dark and all goes wrong,
And clouds hang dull and heavy o'er the land,
And lonesome longings lie about the heart.

Then, by and by, they shape themselves to song ;
And chords awakened by the master hand
Soothe other souls to peace—and this is art.

THE END OF A DREAM.

THE sun was just as bright, perhaps,
    That afternoon in May,
And the meadows just as green, I think,
    As they are there to-day ;
And the sky and sea were just as blue,
    And yet it seemed to me
A cloud was over all the land,
    A storm o'er all the sea.

For we had met there on the shore—
    We two, had met to part—
And the cloud was in my aching brain,
    The storm within my heart ;
And I knew before we met there
    That I could but hear the worst,
Yet when I looked into her face
    I thought my heart would burst.

She was so pale, so beautiful,—
   She spoke so sad and sweet,
Her voice came like the murmur
   Of the waters at our feet;
While the gentle breeze played softly
   With her loosely-prisoned hair;
I took her pure, white hand in mine.
   'Twas cold, and trembled there.

But when I asked if she were cold,
   She only shook her head.
"The day is fair, and I am warm
   Except at heart," she said.
And as she told me of the wrong
   That severed her from me,
I begged her to seek out a home
   With me beyond the sea.

But she gently, firmly answered,
   That her duty was to stay—
That a parent had commanded
   And she could not disobey;
And she told me as we parted,
   That we must not meet again—
The past could only bring regret,
   The present only pain.

And then we kissed and said good-by,
   Just as we used to do.
I saw a tear was in her eye,
   And one was in mine, too.
The pleasant dream is ended now,
   As all dreams end at last.
I know not if my life is worse,
   Or better, for the past!

THE MIRROR.

WITHIN the glass
Our shadows pass,
   Like phantoms one by one,
But in the glass
Our lips may kiss
   No image save their own.

HIS POEM.

HE was a knightly youth of long ago
    Who sallied forth to battle with the world
    And win a laurel wreath—and gaily twirled
His untried lance, and shield that glistened so.
Unwary youth !   Alás, how could he know
    What barriers before him might be hurled :
    And one by one his vanities were furled
Till hope lay dead within his breast ; and lo,
His heart grew faint and faltered in the strife.
  For him would ne'er be woven laurel crown.
    He gave it up, he could no longer cope ;
And only wrote the poem of his life
  In one bright tear, that trickled softly down
    Among the ashes of a blighted hope.

MY TWO POETS.

A PORTRAIT hangs above me as I write—
 A poet's face, done by a poet's hand ;
And both have been my masters, one, my friend ;
 And I have loved them both ; and, oh ! to-night
I love them still, and think perhaps they know,
 For they are dust and ashes long ago.

Yes, I have thought the shades of these dear two
 Must feel the yearning of my hungry heart ;
  The stretching of my arms to the unseen ;
  My gaze into the darkness ; and have been,
 Of my unsated life, the better part.
And I have called as if they really knew—
 Oh, precious thought ! And am I all to blame ?
 And yet—and yet—no answer ever came.

AFTER THE STORM.

A storm swept over the land last night—
   A rush of wind and sweep of rain ;
And ruin and wreck have marked its flight,
   But now, at morn, there is peace again.

Here is a tree laid flat to the grass,
   And here is another twisted and torn ;
But the birds break forth in a song as I pass,
   And my lungs are filled with the breath of morn.

A storm swept over my heart one night—
   A rush of anger—a flood of wrath ;
And its furious flight was marked with blight,
   And wrecks lay thick in its path.

But now, at morn, when the sun in the East
   Is mirrored by every blade of grass,
The winds are stilled, and the floods have ceased,
   And a song breaks forth as I pass.

FROM AFAR.

O-NIGHT a spirit leadeth me
Beyond the land, above the sea—
Amid the mists where memory
    Must pause and grope and seek advice.
Beyond the shore, beyond the wave,
Where memory lingers by the grave
Of babyhood, and lilies bloom
In fadeless glory round the tomb;
    So pure, so fair,
    They blossom there,
    While faint, sweet echoes fill the air,
        Like tinkling chimes from paradise.

Dear mother, as the day wears on,
My heart turns backward toward the dawn,
The fairest hours, the soonest gone,
    And through an atmosphere of dreams
Thy cradle songs I seem to hear,

Thy magic tales still charm my ear,
 And from those rhymes
 And dream-lit times
  A flood of inspiration streams.

Dear father as I wander back
To-night, along the winding track
 Where I have passed
 Until, at last,
  I turn to view the toilsome way,
In many a dim, uncertain place,
When faint and faltering in the race,
 I can but mark,
 Amid the dark,
  Thy reassuring ray,
Thy calm advice, thy quiet grace
  That led me to the day.

Oh, parents, little did I guess
In youth your tender watchfulness ;
 The days of care,
 The hours of prayer,
  The sacrifices made ;
But now, as falls the winter's snow
Upon your heads, ah, well I know

How great the debt of love I owe—
    How little I have paid.

And, as the spirit leadeth me
Beyond the shore, beyond the sea,
Amid the mists afar and dim,
To recollection's utmost rim,
To where the deathless lilies wave
By babyhood's enchanted grave,
    And night and morning meet,
I gather from those blossoms rare
A fadeless wreath, and from the air
Those tinkling, tender chimes that seem
Like music mingling with a dream ;
  And from those chimes
  And dream-lit times
  I weave this simple wreath of rhymes
    And lay it at your feet.

THE WOODMAN'S DREAM.

On the bank of a flowing river,
   Far up 'mid the mountains green,
A woodman sighed for the prairies wide,
   And the cities he ne'er had seen.

Said the woodman, "I'm weary of mountains —
   I am sick of the river's flow;
But lo, I have been so long shut in,
   That I know not where to go."

On the banks of that murmuring river
   He dreamed a wonderful dream;
And an angel came, in an aureate flame,
   And stood by the flowing stream.

And the woodman said, "Oh, angel,
   I am old and the tide runs low,
But I want to go forth to the great, wide earth,
   Oh, show me the way to go.

" I want to behold the cities
  And the glories of other lands ;"
But the angel was gone, and he woke at dawn
  In a city not made with hands.

INFINITY.

BIG fish have little fish
  On which to make their dinners,
And little fish have lesser fish
  And so the thing continners.

Just turn the thing around about
  'Twill work the other way, sir,
For big fish find bigger fish
  To catch 'em every day, sir.

PERSIMMONS.

Oh, it makes no diff'rence whether
We have dark or sunny weather,
Or whether the season's a dry one er a wet,
You can bet your bottom dollar
That the trees along the holler
Will be full of big persimmons, for they've never
failed us yet.

Oh, the corn an' oats an' wheat crop,
Turnips, 'taters an' the beet crop,
Are now an' then a fizzle, an' it makes us swear
an' sweat ; .
But there's one thing we can bank on
That we've never drawed a blank on—
It's the 'simmon crop in Kansas that has never
failed us yet.

When the leaves are fallin', fallin',
  An' departin' birds are callin',
Callin' sof'ly to each other, "It is time for us to
        get;"
  When the year's expirin' ember
  Flings its light along November,
We will gather in our 'simmon crop that never
        failed us yet.

A WORN OUT WOMAN RESTS.

Poor, tired hands that toiled so hard for me, .
   At rest before me, now, I see them lying.
They toiled so hard, and yet we could not see
         That she was dying.

Poor, rough, red hands that drudged the live-
   · long day,
   Still busy when the midnight oil was burning.
Oft toiling on until she saw the gray
         Of day returning.

If I could sit and hold those tired hands,
   And feel the warm life-blood within them beat·
         ing,
And gaze with her across the twilight lands,
         Some whispered words repeating.

I think to-night that I would love her so,
　And I could tell my love to her so truly,
That, e'en though tired, she would not wish to go
　　And leave me thus unduly.

Poor, tired heart, that had so weary grown,
　That death came all unheeded o'er it creeping.
How still it is to sit here all alone
　　While she is sleeping !

Dear, patient heart that deemed the heavy care
　Of drudging household toil its highest duty :
That laid aside its precious yearnings there
　　Along with beauty.

Dear heart and hands, so pulseless still and cold,
　(How peacefully and dreamlessly she's sleep-
　　ing !)
The spotless shroud of rest about them fold
　　And leave me weeping.

THE ANGLER.

The sun looks down on many a stream,
  The stream beholds but one bright sun,
And in a fair reflected beam
  It sparkles till the day is done.

I know beneath that limpid tide,
  In those cool depths, far out of sight,
Uncounted trout and bass abide
  I know, and yet they never bite.

I know this is as fair a spot
  As ever human heart could wish,
And yet the other side, I wot,
  Looks like a better place to fish.

I've said that failure is a crime,
  A culpable, excuseless thing,
And yet I know that I must climb
  The hill path with an empty string.

I know that truth's a jewel bright,
  I know it and I heave a sigh,
To think that I'll go home to-night
  And tell a great, unholy lie.

THE COLLARLESS DOG.

In the mire and the slush, in the grovelling rush
Of the dirtiest street in the city,
A miserable waif, uncared for, unsafe,
Unknown to protection or pity,
I am seeking for bread, to get beatings instead
Or morsels unfit for a hog—
I am leading a life of contemptible strife,
For I'm only a collarless dog.

I skulk, and I hide on the opposite side
Of the street, and I shiver and start
When I see in the distance that bane of existence,
The merciless dog-catcher's cart.
No shelter, no home, and I ceaselessly roam,
The street gamins kick me and flog,
No pity they know for a being so low
As a miserable collarless dog.

Philanthropists, hark to my pitiful bark
As you daintily trip on your way ;
Do you think you'll discover, the city all over,
A being more wretched to-day ?
They only throw stones ! as if skin covered bones
Had feelings no more than a log ;
And little I care, I am used to hard fare
For I'm only a collarless dog.

Full well do I know that I some day shall go
By the route that my brothers have passed ;
For the dog-catcher's cart, and his merciless art
Will win in the struggle at last.
Then, away to the pound, no more to be found
In humanity's bustle and clog,
And a plunge in the river will wind up forever
The woes of a collarless dog.

CONCERNIN' SOME FOLKS.

.

Some folks is allers grumblin', no matter what
    they've got,
A-finding fault with what they have, an' wantin'
    what they've not.
An' you'd think, to hear 'em-kickin' an' a-cussin' of
    their luck,
That the world's a bad investment an' the Lord's
    a-gettin' stuck ;
An' it riles me up to hear 'em a-complainin' all
    the time,
With their measly misconception of the works o'
    the Sublime,
An' it sets me to reflectin' on the merits of the case,
An' a-drawin' of conclusions appertainin' to the
    race ;

Till I've sorter got to thinkin' that it's sinful to
    complain,
That there's jest as much of pleasure as there ever
    was of pain ;
That there ain't no more to cuss about than what
    there is to bless,
An' things are pretty ekally divided up, I guess :
For when you strike a balance 'twixt the shadder
    an' the sun,
The two will allers ekallize when all is said an'
    done ;
An' the world is balanced even, er it wouldn't
    spin aroun',
An' the hills'll fill the hollers when the thing is
    leveled down.
There's another old-time doctrine, an' I've found
    it mighty true,
That you never get a thing without a-losin' some-
    thin' too ;
That there never was a gain without a correspon-
    din' loss ;
That you're not agoin' to wear a crown unless you
    bear a cross.
An' when you see a pint in life, the where you'd
    like to get,

You may make it soon er later, but you'll pay fur
    it, I bet.

A man may get the larnin' of the sciences an' sich,

An' another deal in futures an' may strike it sud-
    den rich,

But the first has lost the peace of mind that once
    he used to feel,

An' the last has lost the relish of the hard-earned,
    honest meal.

An' when you see a feller that has got things ex-
    tra nice,

You can gambol than fur all he's got he's paid
    the market price.

An' if your life was figured out, I'll tell you what,
    my friend,

You'd find it balanced just the same as his'n at
    the end.

Then quit your fool complainin' an' a-studyin'
    how to shirk,

For the time you spend in cussin' you can better
    spend in work.

Things do take on a billious look, at times, I must
    admit,

But a kickin' an' complainin' won't help the thing
    a bit.

An' the clouds that come a driftin' by 'll vanish
     one by one,
An' a-peerin' from behind 'em is the glory of the
     sun.
There's as much of sun as shadder in every drap
     o' dew,
There's as much of day as darkness when you
     take the year all through ;
There's as much of sun as shadder in every human
     heart,
An' of day an' night in every life you'll find an
     ekal part.
An' should there be a residue a-stan'in either way,
The Lord'll make it ekal on the other side, some
     day.

THE BOOK-KEEPER.

All day he toiled with book an' pen
The same as lots of other men.
Sometimes at night the clerks would say,
" Bill Smith, you goin' home to-day ? "
An' Bill 'ud lift his tired face,
An' make a mark to keep his place,
An' sorter sigh, an' say that he
Was ready as he'd ever be,
    He reckoned.

An' years went by, an' seasons flew
An' somehow Bill was never through.
An' when, one day, the Angel came
An' gently whispered William's name,
Bill sorter raised his eyes to look,
A minnit, from his balance book.
" All, right ; I'm comin' now," says he,
" I'm ready as I'll ever be,
    " I reckon."

REVISITED.

Nope, I never was an advercate fer clearin' up
    the lan',
An' I never was in favor of these medders made
    by han';
If them folks 'at live back yander air so bent on
    raisin' hay,
They hed better sell an' come out West is all
    I've got to say;
An' they'd better move to Kansas, where there's
    miles of verdant sod,
Than to waste the'r time a-tryin' to improve the
    works o' God.

Why, las' fall I went to Hampshire, just to see
    the brook ag'in

Where I use' to fish in boyhood's days—'twas
    night when I got in—

An' I hadn't seen ol' Hampshire's hills fer forty
    years er more,

So I riz at day nex' mornin and surveyed the
    lan'scape o'er ;

An' I looked across the valley jes as fur as I c'u'd
    see,

An' I saw the *grass a-wavin' wher' the timber use'
    to be.*

An' when I went down to the brook the water
    wasn't there,

An' the music of its meller voice hed vanished
    in the air ;

For they've cut off all the ellums, jes to put the
    lan' in hay,

An' the sun hes burnt the water tell it's all b'iled
    away ;

An' when I saw the pore ol' brook, I set down by
    its side,

An' I guess I could'nt help it, fer I jes broke
    down an' cried.

Nope, I never was an advercate of clearin' up
    the lan',
An' I never was in favor of these medders made
    by han';
So I guess I'll stay in Kansas jes' a-turnin' up
    the sod,
Where the sun-flowers air a-bloomin' by the
    medder-lands o' God.

A WEARY PHILOSOPHER.

He sleeps.
Calmly he lies,
His tired eyes
    Forever closed.
Such perfect rest
In that calm breast
    Never reposed.

Worn with the strife,
And burdens of life,
    Soundly he slumbers ;
Heedless that I,
Standing near by,
    Murmur these numbers.

Tireless he pondered
While the world wondered
  At his seclusion.
Problems that vexed him,
Long years perplexed him,
  Now find solution.

Calmly he left us,
That which bereft us,
  Came without warning.
Dreaming they thought him,
While darkness had brought him
  Another morning.

AN ANSWER TO "LITTLE BOY BLUE."

[TO EUGENE FIELD.]

If Little Boy Blue had played out in the dirt
    With a top and a twisted string,
In cotton trousers and checkered shirt,
    And swung on a grapevine swing ;
Then the little toy dog, so bright and new,
    And the soldier so "passing fair"
Would never have yearned for the "Little Boy
    Blue"
    Who kissed them and put them there."

For a Little Boy Blue must get spattered with
    mud
    And wade in the branch, and swim ;
The splash in the water will quicken his blood,
    And dirt is a boon to him !
Oh, pent-up nurs'ries and toys so new !
    Oh, graves ! and the dumb despair
Of the hearts that ache for a Little Boy Blue,
    When we've kissed him and laid him there !

PADEREWSKI.

I HEARKENED last night to his playing—
    This poet from over the sea,
And the grace of that marvelous music
    Has ministered unto me.

'Twas a cadence of angel voices
    And it strengthened my spirit like wine,
As he poured out his soul in its message,
    And blended it into mine.

I know very little of music,
    And I care not for technical worth,
But I know that the sound of that singing
    Has fitted me better for earth.

LE ROI EST MORT.

It is the hour of the expiring Year.
　His garnered days are gathered in the sheaf ;
　The glory and the grandeur and the grief
Are ended now—and only death is here.
Tread lightly, and let fall, perchance, a tear
　For this poor king whose reign was all too brief ;
　Whose splendor has become a withered leaf—
A flickering candle, and a waiting bier.

But hark ! the stroke is on the midnight hour !
　See ! he is clutching, gasping, he is gone !
　　This infant at the door ! what doth he bring ?
Ring out ! Ring out ! from every town and tower.
　Ring out the bells until the break of dawn,
　　And shout, "The king is dead ! Long live
　　　the king."

UNBIDDEN.

I gave up making verses long ago—
   I said, " For me it is a useless thing,
   For fate hath clipped my roving fancy's wing,
And quenched the flame—it can no longer glow."
Ah, foolish heart !   How little do we know—
   The captive bird will still, unbidden, sing,
   And though upon my harp is snapped each
      string,
As well to bid the river not to flow ;
   For when fair Nature's beauties I behold,
   Or dream upon the days that once have been,
The spark that I believed was dead and cold
   Doth glow and burn and burst to flame again ;
And words that I can scarce believe my own
Leap to my lips—I cannot keep them down.

WHAT THE WINDS SAID.

OH, a wind came whispering out of the west
    And these are the words that it said to me.
" Of all life's treasures love is the best,"
Oh, a wind came whispering out of the west,
    All up from a summer sea.

A wind came whispering out of the east
    And these are the words that it murmured low,
" Of all life's treasures wealth is the least,"
Oh, the winds came out of the west and the east
    And they told the truth, I know.

THAT RED-HAIRED GIRL.

THAT red-haired girl, with azure eye—
Just now I saw her tripping by !
        What makes me start and tremble so ?
        'Tis not that red-haired girl, I know !
And yet, somehow, I heave a sigh.

For she is fair and tall, while I,
Alas, am dark, and thin, and dry ;
        What stuff is this I've writ ! but oh,
                That red-haired girl !

What odds to me, you say ?   Oh, my,
How hard it is to tell a lie
        When one beholds that throat of snow—
        And eyes grow dim, and pulses go !
God bless my soul's delight !   Who ?   Why,
                That red-haired girl.

.

A CHRISTMAS WAIF.

I WILL sing you a song of the long ago,
  A tale of a little child
Who came one night through the sleet and snow
To a Christmas feast in the long ago,
  When the night was dark and wild.

Who crept away from its wretched home
  To the lights across the way,
Where the warmth and bloom of the rich man's
      room
Dispelled from his little breast the gloom
  That had filled it all that day.

And he clambered up to the casement wide,
  And drank in the vision fair,
Of the rich man's hearth and the rich man's pride,
And the happy children that side by side
  Were treading the dances there.

And he soon forgot the pitiless storm
   As he hearked to that merry din ;
He felt not the blast on his shrinking form,
And his brain grew light, and his heart grew warm
   From the light and the warmth within.

And softly over him slumber crept,
   And softly the glow and the gleam
Faded out from the weary eyes that slept,
Transformed, as the storm unheeded swept,
   Into a wonderful dream.

Where he floated away on a cloud of gold,
   Over a silver sea,
To a magical island where hunger and cold
Can never be found and have never been told ;
Where summer eternal its glories unfold,
   And sorrow will never be.

And down to the shore of that mystical isle
   A beautiful angel came,
And she held out her hand, and she seemed to
      smile
To welcome the waif to that wonderful isle,
   And tenderly called his name.

Then gladly he followed, and hand in hand,
  Those blossoming fields they trod,
Till lo ! in the distance a cherubic band,
Surrounded the King of that glorious land,
And the angel whispered that held his hand,
  "Thou, too, art a lamb of God."

     *   *   *   *   *   *

And Christmas morning came, cold and bright,
  For the storm with the night had fled, .
And there in the casement, crowned with light,
And robed in a shroud of spotless white,
  A little child lay dead.

THE FIRST CHRISTMAS EVE.

On Judah's plain one winter night
   A message to some shepherds came ;
A star appeared, supremely bright,
   And rested over Bethlehem,
While glory shone around.
Prostrate upon the ground
   They fell, and then a voice,
From out the flood of radiance, said
" Fear not, for I have come to bid
   Mankind rejoice."

And from the vaults of heaven high,
The shepherds heard this joyous cry,
   " The child is born,
Haste thee and follow yonder star
That guideth onward from afar,
   Nor wait for morn.

" Within a manger thou shalt find
The infant ruler of mankind,
     Jesus, thy king."
And then a fair celestial throng,
United in a joyous song
     Of welcoming.

" Glory to God," the angels sang,
" Peace and good will," the heavens rang,
     " To all the earth."
" The Lord has come, the king of kings
A heavenly host rejoicing sings
     To greet His birth."

To teach mankind a better way,
To light them with a purer ray
     The Savior came.
He came to be their patient guide,
For love of them He lived,—and died
     A death of shame.

Still through the night,
His holy light
     Is guiding them.
Still beams the star
That rose afar
     O'er Bethlehem.

THE MYSTICAL SEA.

Oh love, I am wandering back to-day
  Through the valleys of memory ;
They lie betwixt mountains far away—
The mountains of Hope and of Youth are they,
And I'm dreaming again of that night, to-day,
  By the mystical southern sea.

Oh, love, I loved you that far-off night !
  By the mystical southern sea.
The breeze was light and the stars were bright,
And the sea-gulls flashed in their circling flight,
As we sat alone on that far-off night,
  When you whispered your love for me.

Oh, I kissed your lips and I clasped your hands,
  By that mystical southern sea,
While softly the waves were kissing the sands,
And ships went a-sailing to distant lands,
As I kissed your lips and I clasped your hands,
  When you whispered your love to me.

Oh, love, a storm has swept the shore
  Of that mystical southern sea ;
The waves still kiss as they kissed before ;
But the ships that sailed will return no more
And the youth and the love and the hopes of yore
  Will never come back to me,—
            Ah, me,
  Will never come back to me.

THE THREE CARAVELS.

Full far I've searched, through many climes,
For pregnant theme and dulcet rhymes;
To sing the day and suit the times
　　I've sought the country over;
Three ships that sail before the breeze
From Spanish main to Southern seas—
To anchor in the Antilles,
　　Are all that I discover.

Three little ships that long ago
Forgot the billow and the blow,
By worm, and wind, and wave laid low
　　On ocean's briny bottom.
Who knows beneath what tropic sky,
And sapphire sea their ashes lie?
Who asks of wherefore, whence, and why,
　　Since Davy Jones has got 'em?

Now, having sought for rhymes that ring—
For thoughts that throb, and words that sing—
My caravels are taking wing,
   I ask that you shall heed 'em.
Gone! did I say? Aye, dead and gone,
No more their sails shall fleck the dawn,
But mark, their souls go sailing on!
   'Tis LOVE—and PEACE—and FREEDOM.

And love sails first through all the world!
A bark of gold with decks empearled—
Its snowy canvas all unfurled—
   Its coffers jewel-laden.
The banner-ship of all mankind!
Its pilot old, and deaf, and blind,
Yet braving reef, and wave, and wind,
   For eager youth and maiden.

Fair ship, that finds on many seas
A welcome tide and wafting breeze,
Press on with sweet discoveries,
   Thy priceless burden bearing!
How fair she rides each foamy crest!
Still sailing to the west—the west!
And finds at last in every breast
   A little rest from faring.

But see !   Another vessel comes !
With flying flags and throbbing drums ;
Above its bow the tempest hums—
      While cannons belch and thunder.
'Tis Freedom ! and its turbid track
Is strewn with dead, and red, and rack,
Yet onward sweeps and turns not back
      Though nations pause and wonder.

Avenging bark, sail on—sail on !
Till every throne is overthrown—
Till men shall rise and claim their own
      From tyrant and invader.
Till Freedom's blessed name shall roll
Through every clime—to every soul—
From heaven to earth—from pole to pole—
      From Zenith unto Nadir !

Lo ! wind and wave once more are stirred,
And hearts, grow faint with hope deferred,
Leap high, as, like a timid bird,
      The bark of Peace is sighted.
A white-winged dove,—oft' beaten back—
That follows ever in the track
Of Freedom, and with turn and tack
      Bears on to hearts united.

Sweet ship of Peace ! thy lines are cast
Where storm is done and strife is past—
Where tyranny has breathed its last—
        And slave has burst his fetter ;
Thy freight is Progress ; and thy way
Is lighted by the living ray
Of heaven's smile, and day by day,
        The world shall know thee better.

Thus have I sought for rhymes that ring,
For thoughts that tell, and themes that sing,
And lo ! my barks have taken wing,
        I ask that you shall speed 'em.
Dead, did I say ?   Their ashes lie
Low neath a southern sea and sky,
But still their souls go sailing by—
        Man's love, and peace, and freedom.

Sail on !   Sail on !   My vessels three,
Through all the centuries to be—
Till hearts awake and tongues are free
        Wherever word is spoken !
Till Bigotry shall cease to blight--
And Zeal at last shall wed with Right—
Till Love and Truth shall win the fight—
        And Peace shall reign unbroken !

TWO OF US.

I go from the hills at break of day
　To my daily toil in the busy town ;
I meet another upon the way,
　And he comes up as I go down.

He comes from the city to dig in the hills ;
　I go from the hills to dig in town ;
He carries his mattock, I my books,
　As he comes up and I go down.

We two are strangers, and yet we nod
　And smile to each other upon the way ;
We two are toilers for daily bread,
　Going forth to dig at the break of day.

At evening time when our work is done,
　And silence falls on the busy town,
We meet again, and we say "good-night,"
　As I come up and he goes down.

I come from the city to rest in the hills ;
  He goes from the hills to rest in town ;
Two weary toilers who say good-night
  As one goes up and the other down.

TO A MOUNTAIN SUMMIT, USED AS A PAPER WEIGHT.*

Thou who a million centuries hath been
An index of th' illimitable God —
With tip-toe on the everlasting hills
And finger touching the eternal blue--
To what strange uses art condemned to-day ;

Reft from thy ancient friend, the far horizon,
To range beside a score of tinsel gems ;
Shut out from heaven, and all the smile of God—
To bask in mortal favor, and become
The tolerated trifle of a king !

*The German Emperor uses as a paper-weight on his writing-
desk the summit of one of the highest mountains of Africa. Dr.
Buchner, an African traveler of some fame, broke the piece of
rock from the highest point of Mount Kilimandjaro, which is on
German-African ground, and presented it to the Emperor.

HALF-WAY.

THE years that steal our youth away
  Come drifting on—come drifting on
Like snowflakes that endure a day
  And then are gone.

     *   *   *   *

Upon the hearth is blazing bright
  An open fire—I sit and dream,
And think how far into the night
  And storm, its radiations stream.

And lo, within my heart, to-night,
  The flame of youth flares up once more,
To shed a gleam of ruddy light
  Through all the dark that lies before.

And all the lost come back once more,
  And all the dead things live again,
And footsteps echo on the floor,
  And faces press against the pane.

And oh, I try so hard to catch
  A whisper from the forms that pass,
To touch the hand that lifts the latch—
  The lips that tremble on the glass.

And seek to check the rising tears
  For sweet dead joys, and loved ones gone,
For memories that like the years
  Come drifting on—come drifting on.

    *   *   *   *

My fire burns low, but through the gloom
  Comes stealing in the gray of dawn.
The shadows skurry from the room
  Till all are gone.

And morn is here—the storm is past,
  The room is filled with rosy day ;
But on my head is drifting fast
  The snow that never melts away.

PASTELS.

A MORNING.

A WAVERING, misty sweep of greenish gray,
A sullen landscape and the flying clouds,
All gray and white,—like parti-colored shrouds—
A chill east wind, a sobbing drift of rain,
A heart that wakes to dull, returning pain
And so is ushered in another day.

AN EVENING.

A DARKENING waste of shadows, sombre brown :
A line of lurid crimson far away—
The waning edge of the departing day.
A row of poplars, black against the west :
A moaning wind, a heart that sighs for rest ;
And so another weary day goes down.

FATE'S ALCHEMY.

SHE was born to serve the muses, but she wedded
    with a clown,
And the drudgery of living filled her life and
    dragged her down.

She was hungry for life's treasures—she had
    dreams of fame and honor,
But they crumbled into ashes as her burdens
    weighed upon her:

But she wrote one little poem with a touch di-
    vinely human;
And it bore a holy message to the soul of one
    lost woman.

BEYOND.

I have been told
There is a land of sweet tranquility,
Apart from life, and from life's sorrows free,
And often in my dreams I seem to see
 It's fields of fadeless green :
A place where deathless roses'bud and bloom
A land of light ; and yet a vail of gloom
Surrounds it and conceals it, while the tomb
 Is but a gate, the earth and it between.

I only know
We reach its dusky portals soon or late,
And at the gloomy entrance trembling wait
Till we are summoned through that silent gate
 Which none repass—whence never word
  can come.
Ah, anxiously I watch a dying friend
And follow with him to the very end,
Then, as I feel him drifting from me, bend
To catch a glimpse or whisper from beyond,
 But all is dark and dumb.

"WEEVILY WHEAT."

Say, Joe, do you remember the days we lived on
    Rollin's prairie,
Content with our simple country ways and our
    sweethearts Sue and Mary?
And those "kissin' parties" we used to have, and
    the game about the barley
And weevily wheat, with its queer old song about
    the cake for Charlie?

  "O, I'll have none of your weevily wheat,
    And I'll have none of your barley,
  O, I'll have none of your weevily wheat
    To bake a cake for Charlie."

And do you remember (I'm sure you do) that glo-
    rious summer weather,
When you and I with Mary and Sue went pick-
    ing plums together?
And how at dusk as we loitered home through
    fields of ripened barley,
We sang the song of "Weevily Wheat" and
    baked the cake for Charley?

  "O, Charlie he's a nice young man,
    Charlie he's a dandy;
  And Charlie loves to kiss the girls
    Whenever they come handy."

Alas, dear Joe, for you and me those happy days
    are over,
For Mary's now beyond the sea and Sue beneath
    the clover:
But sometimes when the days are dark and the
    skein of life is snarly,
I think once more of "Weevily Wheat" and the
    cake we baked for Charlie.

  "Then I'll have none of your weevily wheat,
    And I'll have none of your barley;
  O, I'll have none of your weevily wheat
    To bake a cake for Charlie."

A GHOST.

O'er this undulating prairie,
  Long ago,
Mighty waters marched with weary
  Ebb and flow.

Stately ships, perhaps, did wander
  Back and forth,
Mighty ice-flows drift and thunder
  From the North.

Now, where rolled that restless ocean,
  Long ago,
Tides of green, with ceaseless motion,
  Meet and flow.

And this gentle, mystic murmur
  Of the dawn
Is the voice of billows firmer
  That are gone.

And the wraith of that old billow
  Is the haze,
Floating softly through the mellow
  Autumn days.

Amethystine, when the golden
  Sun is low,
As the waves were in that olden
  Long ago.

Mighty plain ! where greenly waving
  Waters meet,
Thou art still an ocean, laving
  At my feet !

A GENIUS.

BILL MacGAVERN was a "genius," in a quiet sort
of way ;
Some fine morning he'd be famous (so his mother
used to say.)
He could fix a clock, and fiddle, and a lot of other
things,
And he made himself a "gitar," and could twang
upon the strings.
He could pick out "Annie Laurie," and the chords
of "Belle Mahone,"
And would sit and sing at evening in a soothing
undertone,
With his dreamy gaze directed to a pale senescent
star,
While he milked the mournful music from his
primitive guitar.

Well, the years went by, and somehow Bill re-
    mained about the same,
Though his mother died believing he was on the
    road to fame.
Bill was full of dreams and notions, but achieve-
    ments seemed to lag ;
Bill was fond of Alice Holeman, but he married
    'Mantha Bragg.
Still he picks out "Annie Laurie," and the chords
    of " Belle Mahone,"
And he sings them to the babies in a soothing
    undertone ;
And perhaps, sometimes, at evening, as he twangs
    his old guitar,
William's vision is directed to a pale senescent
    star.

THE PARISH SCHOOL.

Two little nuns are teaching school
  Near by on Cosy Street ;
I pass each morning, as a rule,
  And now and then we meet.

The humble house is small and low ;
  Its walls are rude and bare ;
And yet I loiter by, for, oh,
  It seems so peaceful there !

I never liked to go to school ;
  I always rather play ;
I hated any kind of rule,
  And sometimes ran away :

But when I pass that little door,
   And breathe that holy air,
I want to be a boy once more,
   And learn my lessons there.

Oh, little nuns, with wimples white,
   And hearts of purest gold,
My soul is troubled sore to-night,
   My heart is growing cold.

Oh, little nuns of sable dress,
   And souls of drifting snow,
Teach me the way of righteousness,
   And I can learn, I know.

THE WILD SUNFLOWER.

At early dawn, like soldiers in their places,
  Rank upon rank the golden sunflowers stand ;
Gazing toward the east with eager faces,
  Waiting until their god shall touch the land
To life and glory, longingly they wait—
These voiceless watchers at the morning's gate.

Dawn's portals tremble silently apart ;
  Far to the east, across the dewy plain,
A glory kindles, that in every heart
    Finds answering warmth, and kindles there
        again ;
While rapture beams from every radiant face
Now softly glowing with supernal grace.

And all day long this silent worship keeps ;
   And as their god moves grandly down the west,
From every stem a lengthening shadow creeps
   Toward the east—ah, then they love him best,
And watch till every lingering ray is gone,
Then slowly turn to greet another dawn.

WISHING FOR STARS.

[TO MY LITTLE FRIEND, CORINNE COSTON.]

"Oh, I wish 'at I had dess a bushel of gold
    To buy all the stars in the sky,
For nen I'd be good an' my ma wouldn't scold
    Cause I's tired of my play-fings an' cry.
I'd stwing 'em all up on a gweat, long stwing
    Dess like little beadies, you know ; "
                Oh, dear little Prue,
                There are others, like you,
Who want all the stars in a row,
                Little girl,
    All the beautiful stars in a row.

There are others, to-night, gazing up at the blue
  And yearning for gold, with a sigh ;
They want to buy stars, and like you, little Prue,
  Grow tired of their play-things and cry.
I, too, I confess, have a weakness for stars
  And would like them all strung in a row,
      For I gave all my toys
      To some bad little boys
And they've broken them, now, I know,
      Little girl,
  They've broken my toys, I know.

Some night when I enter the valley of dreams
  That lies in the kingdom of nod,
Where flitaways dance on the silvery beams
  Sifting down from the lantern of God,
I will capture the daintiest fairy of all
  And send her far up in the blue,
      On her humming-bird wings,
      With a lot of long strings
To gather the stars on for you,
      Little girl,
  To string all the stars for you.

THAT MYSTERY.

When e'er I try to reason out
    The life that is and is to be,
The only thing I bring about
    Is reason's cold philosophy.

The cradle stands upon the shore
    Of that dark sea, whose restless wave
Lies close behind, and just before
    Is tossing up against the grave.

We drift out from that dim unknown
    Up to the shore of life, and then,
Ere long, we shape a bark, and soon
    Drift out upon that sea again.

The world is but a tiny isle
  Wherein to make a moment's stay—
We pause and fret a little while
  And then pursue our onward way.

We come, we go, who knoweth more?
  From what dim region were we borne?
And who shall say what other shore
  Our bark may touch ere its return?

DEACON PETER'S JASPER.

JASPER PETERS was a "shiftless sort of fellow"
    people said,
Wouldn't work if he could help it and just laid
    around and read ;
Always tinkering with sleight-of-hand and chem-
    icals and such,
And the neighbors " 'lowed " that Jasper wouldn't
    " ever 'mount to much ; "
Though they did admit that he was " mighty
    clever doin' tricks,"
And they wondered how he managed to make
    fire and water mix :
Till one morning when the Deacon said that Jap.
    had run away,
Then they sighed and kinder smiled and rather
    hoped that he would stay.

And they said twas "jes' like Jasper" when they
    learned at last that he
Was a sailor on a whaler in a far-off southern
    sea.

Seven months the lapping waters lulled the
    wanderer to sleep,
Then a storm swept o'er the ocean and the temp-
    est rent the deep ;
And his shipmates and the gallant ship went
    down to rise no more,
But our lucky hero drifted to a tropic island shore ;
Where a lot of dusky damsels found him lying
    on the beach,
Freighted heavily with water and incapable of
    speech ;
And they hastily conveyed him to their habita-
    tion where
They relieved him of his cargo and inflated him
    with air ;
And they tenderly propelled him through a rack-
    siege of croup,
And they bled him and they fed him and they
    fattened him for soup ;

And at length, when his condition was consid-
    ered quite the thing,
They conveyed him as a present to his majesty,
    the king.

But Jap. rose before the elders of that sea-encir-
    cled land,
And he threw them into spasms with some feats
    of sleight-of-hand ;
Till those semi-naked people swarmed about him
    where he trod,
And went down before his magic and adored him
    as a god ;
And at last in open council they avowed that it
    was plain
That the sea had sent a ruler and that Jasper
    was to reign ;
And removed his predecessor with a diplomatic
    coup,
For they deftly smote his head off and converted
    him to soup,
Thus assuring to our hero the essentials of suc-
    cess,
And, with greatness thrust upon him, Jap. was
    bound to acquiesce ;

And they chose him many consorts from the fair-
     est in the land,
And among them were the maidens that had
     found him on the sand.
Thus the youth, for whose infirmities the neigh-
     bors used to groan,
Rules a race of rugged warriors and has rock-
     ers on his throne.

FIRST SNOW-FALL.

THE sun that dim November day
Had failed to kiss the clouds away
From quiet Nature's furrowed face,
Where autumn tears had left their trace.

And, by and by, on fields of brown
The feathered flakes came floating down
From Heaven to this world of ours,
Like spirits of departed flowers.

And fast and faster through the night,
Till Morn arose on meadows white,
And o'er the landscape lightly stepped
Where tired Nature, smiling, slept.

THE RHYME OF THE SPANISH NEEDLE.

WHEN the sunflowers are a-dying on the hollow
    and the hill,
And the golden-rod is budding, kind of waiting
    like until
Frosty mornings have unfolded all its regimental
    plumes,
There's a little inter-regnum when the Spanish-
    needle blooms.

Now the nights are growing chilly and the morn-
    ings cool and calm,
And the days are sweet and sunny filled with
    Nature's pungent balm ;
There's a rare intoxication in those aromatic
    fumes
When the sunflower is a-dying and the Spanish-
    needle blooms.

There's a mist upon the meadow in these dreamy
    autumn days,
And the world is bathed at evening in an ame-
    thystine haze ;
There's a joy in mere existence that the raptured
    soul consumes
When the golden-rod is budding and the Span-
    ish-needle blooms.

Oh, the fallow fields of autumn they are full of
    drifting gold !
And 'tis there I seek for treasure like a cavalier
    of old ;
For the jewels of her sunsets, for her casket of
    perfumes,
For the priceless joy of living when the Spanish-
    needle blooms.

FRAGMENT.

THE prayer is said, the hymn is sung,
  The calm dead face from us is hid—
The solemn knell is sadly rung,
  The clods fall on the coffin lid.

It is an autumn afternoon—
  The blue-fringed gentian nods its head
Above the open grave that soon
  Will rise between us and the dead.

I gaze upon the heap of ground
  That hides my last, my dearest friend—
This tearful throng, this silent mound,
  Is this the end, is this the end?

IT HAPPENED THUS.

He was an artist; patiently he toiled
To gain the heights that glimmered from afar,
And with the years had won a partial fame.

She was an actress, young and very fair,
Wending her way along a quiet path,
Toward a height of which she, likewise, dreamed.

One day they met, I know not when nor how,
(They hardly knew, themselves, in after days)
They met to love, with that great, deathless love
That Earth conceives in an embrace with Heaven,
And brings to birth when e'er the two fair parts
Of one great Soul shall touch upon her breast.
To love with them were life—to part were death.

So, when a parent hand, impelled by pride
And mother-worship for an only child—
A hand that sought to clasp a gilded crown
For that fair head—was laid between their hearts,
The sun went out, and darkness settled down
On those two lives, as o'er a sunless sea.

They met again. "My life is naught," he said,
"Nor yet is mine," she answered, "let us die."
How sweet to him that proffered boon of death !
To die with her, the thought had been his own
By day and night ; and so the tryst was made.

That night, a voice beneath her window called,
"Art ready, Emilie ?" And her voice replied,
"Yes, Gustave, ready." Then a shot rang out,
And answering from above, another came
That seemed its echo in the silent night.

And then came hurrying feet and startled cries,
And lights were brought ; and one lay on the
        ground
With face turned upward to the flaring lamps,
And prating crowd, and from his temple flowed
A crimson stream that swept his life away.

Above, they found the other ; robed in white,
Upon her bed she lay as one asleep.
Pinned to her breast a spray of heliotrope,
But not a stain to mark the fatal wound.

And when they parted back the snowy robe
From her sweet loveliness, they found no blood ;
Only a tiny hole in that fair breast,
Through which the fretted soul had slipped away
To seek its mate beyond our narrow rim.

GABRIEL.

A CHRISTMAS TALE.

TWAS early autumn. On the orchard slope
The golden fruit, and that of ruddy red
Hung thickly on the farmer's apple trees ;
And merry voices echoed all around
Of those who gathered in the ripened fruit.
The farmer's son, young Gabriel Worthington,
Worked with the rest, the gayest of them all.
He was a handsome youth, of barely twenty ;
Graceful and strong and fair to gaze upon,
And farmer Worthington—a stern, proud man,
Of iron will, and temper violent—
Beheld his noble boy with silent pride.
He seldom praised him ; such was not his way,
But those who knew him well, were well aware

That there was naught to him like Gabriel.
His only living boy, and when at birth
The life of the young mother had gone out
Upon the ebb-tide of an unknown sea,
The father's love had centered all in him.

   And as young Gabriel grew, a romping child,
The father took him with him to his work ;
And on the hill-side where the orchard grew
He made his favorite play-ground.   There in
          autumn
He loved to play among the laden trees,
Tossing the golden apples here and there
In sportive mischief.
                  Rolling on the ground
Upon the clover and luxuriant grass.
But, sometimes, when the farmer chided him
For bruising apples, tossing them about,
Or for some other childish thoughtlessness,
His little face would flush with angry looks,
And angry fire dart from the childish eyes,
And angry words leap from the childish lips
Of this young rebel who inherited
His father's temper and his iron will.
His father seeing this and knowing well

How useless it would be to try to break
That which he knew was bred into the bone,
Refrained from rousing up that latent fire,
Thinking that it might smoulder out and die.

And so he grew in years and went to school,
And was a handsome youth, and fair, and tall,
And forward in his studies ; and as well
Was skilled in every kind of boyish sport.
And farmer Worthington looked on with pride
And loved him all the more, but, being proud,
He could not show the depths of his affection.
And Gabriel loved his father and his home,
But, being like his father, did not tell
How much he loved ; and so the years went on.
The rest of us, a merry, romping crew,
The offspring of our father's second union,
Regarded him as nobler flesh and blood,
And worshipped him although we feared him ; he
Was always kind to us and made us toys,
And told us tales, and taught us childish games ;
And taught us lessons from the well-worn books
Which he had mastered.
                    Thus was he the king,
That with firm kindness ruled our little band,
And every word from him, to us, was law.

And so the years went on, and he was sent
A little distance to a higher school,
And, graduating there, came home at last
More manly and more polished in his ways,
More handsome, and we loved him all the more.
And all the while a slumbering lion lay
Within his youthful breast, which not aroused
Was thought to have gone hence, or to have died
Of inanition in his childhood years.
And even he knew not that it was there.
But there were those who knew the father well,
And knew the son as well from boyhood up,
Who shook their heads, and said the time would
        come
When Gabriel and his father, face to face,
Should stand in anger.
                Little did they know
How soon the time would come, but much they
        feared.

And now 'twas apple harvest, and the fruit
Was almost gathered, and the gatherers
Were making merry as they neared the end.
And Gabriel laughed and joked with all the rest,
And led the sport as he had led the work.

Perhaps he grew a little careless, too,
As one is apt to do in midst of mirth,
For something happened that the father saw,
Something about the sorting of the fruit
That did not please him, and he rashly spoke
In sharp reproof to Gabriel, who replied
With words as sharp, that it was not his work.
To which the father answered, that his work
Should be to see that other's was done well.
Then Gabriel's quick retort was like the flash
Of fire, when flint strikes steel, and in his breast
A wave of anger rose, that rushing on
Swept all before it, and, with mighty roar,
The sleeping lion was aroused at last.

And furious words that could not be recalled,
Were uttered by the father and the son
In heat of anger, till, at last, the boy,
In livid passion, vowed that he would go,
And leave his father's roof forevermore.
At which the father, white with awful rage,
Bade him to quit his sight at once, and swore
He ne'er would see his face in life again.
And Gabriel turned without another word
And left the spot ; and then for many days

We of the younger brood in secret mourned,
Fearing to let our father see our grief;
While he was only silent, and more stern;
Although at night we sometimes told each other
That he expected Gabriel might come back,
And that he yearned for him in silent grief.

But days ran into weeks, and weeks to months,
And months to years, and Gabriel did not come.
Until at last we seldom spoke his name,
And, child-like, half forgot him.
                              So it is
With one who dies, and passes from our ken;
A little while we mourn for him, and then
His place is filled up by the crowding years.
But there was one, his father, unto whom
The years brought no forgetfulness, we saw
His hair grow grayer quickly, and we knew
That in his heart he mourned his absent boy,
And ever looked and longed for his return.

And, meantime, where was Gabriel?   He had
        gone
Forth from the home he loved, in furious wrath,
And blind with fury scarce knew where he fled

Till he was far from his paternal roof.
He never thought of turning back, not he ;
His father's pride and will were in he breast,
And on he hurried toward the distant town.
He had a little money in his purse,
And with it he would go into the world
And seek his fortune and return no more.
The mellow shadows of the autumn eve
Began to fall around him, and his wrath
Was wearing off, but, greater than his wrath,
His pride remained and drove him on and on.

So Gabriel went out into the world,
And for a while he drifted here and there,
Working as he could find the work to do,
Waiting till opportunity should afford
A place for him in life where he might win
Something beyond a meager livelihood.
And when one morning, after many years,
He learned of an exploring expedition
Then forming to invade the arctic seas,
He never paused or hesitated once,
But sought the leaders of that gallant crew,
And volunteered his life and services.
And when they looked into his handsome face,

And marked the grace and strength of his young
      limbs,
And heard the daring echo in his voice,
They gladly numbered him among their band,
And promised him a place where he might win
With strength, and courage, and achieve pro-
      motion.
And Gabriel, glad that all went well at last,
Yet yearning always for the ones he loved,
Now thought once more upon his childhood's
      home,
And longed to see the faces there again
Before he sailed away from them forever

   And thinking much, at last resolved to go
And look once more upon the old home place.
For it is Christmas-tide, and well he knows
That all the living ones will gather there,
And he can steal up to the house at eve
And watch the faces round the open fire
Unknown to them, unseen by any there.

So Gabriel goes ; and coming to the town
That lies the nearest to his father's farm,
Decides that he will walk the well-known road,
Wherein he sees some changes have been made,

And, changed himself, he fears not recognition.
By nightfall he can reach the hill-side farm,
Then, hurrying back, can catch the morning train
And none will be the wiser for his call.

To-morrow will be Christmas day ; how well
He loved this time in merry by-gone years,
And hung his stocking by the open fire
And found it always filled on Christmas morn.
He wonders if the children all are there—
His little sisters must be women now—
And o'er him comes a swift and strong desire
To be with them, and in his home once more.
And in his heart is formed a half resolve
To cast aside all bitterness, and ask
Forgiveness of his father ; but his pride
Rises in strong rebellion, and the thought
Is banished from his breast, and then he feels
That he is but a stranger in this place,
At home, and yet in homeless solitude,
And sadness settles o'er his lonely heart.

A monotone of clouds o'ercasts the sky,
Thick, and unbroken, save where one light spot
Reveals the sun in dim obscurity.

The atmosphere is damp and full of gloom,
As if oppressed by heavy weight of woe,
And snow-flakes seem about to form and fall.
The earth is bare, as yet the winter snows
Have held aloof ; but Gabriel is aware
From all the signs that now a storm is nigh ;
And Christmas morn will find the roadway white,
And sleigh-bells jingling on the frosty air
Will tell the merry joys of Christmas-tide.
But little cares he for the coming storm ;
The nights are long, and well he knows the way
And only cares to reach the town by dawn.
The melancholy rustling of dry leaves,
The cast-off summer mantle of the forest,
That spreads in sombre glory o'er the ground,
Now crackling neath the traveler's hurrying feet,
Is all the sound that breaks upon the air,
And filled with thoughts of home, and of the past,
In silent sadness Gabriel hurries on
And vanishes amid the gathering gloom.

———

'Tis morning ! and the tardy winter's sun
Slow rises to illuminate the world.
All nature is enwrapped in ermine robes
That glisten in the sun in dazzling splendor,

As if incrusted with the richest gems.
The trees are dressed as if by fairy hands,
And elfins seem to play at hide and seek
Between the boughs, that bending 'neath the
       weight
Of their rich dress, soft touch the farmer's head ;
And as he gently jars the laden branches
A little avalanche comes tumbling down
Upon his coat, and hat, and decks them out
Till he appears a hoary winter's king.

  He lightly brushes off the feathery stuff,
And bending forward, pushes through the drifts,
Plowing a pathway toward the stable door
Whence comes a coaxing whinney that denotes
His faithful horse awaits its morning meal.
Then, just before the slatted stable door,
He finds a drift much larger than the rest,
And wading through it stumbles o'er a form
That lies unseen beneath the heaped up snow.
He stops to see what hidden obstacle
Has blocked his path, and, brushing off the snow,
The figure of a man reveals itself,
Frozen and stark with face turned to the ground.
The farmer wondering much who it can be,

That seeks out such a place in such a night
When warmth and shelter are so close at hand,
Lays hold upon the rigid form and turns
The dead face upward to the morning light.
Then down upon his knees he trembling sinks,
And uttering one wild cry of "GABRIEL!"
He falls prostrate across the frozen man.

Yes, it was Gabriel; he had wandered back
To view once more the place where he was born;
To take a last, a long and lingering look
Before he sailed away forevermore.
Perhaps he stood outside the window-pane
Gazing so long at those dear ones within,
That he was chilled, and stiff, and when he went
His eyes were blinded, and his limbs benumbed:
And stumbling back into night and gloom
And blinding snow he lost his path, and then
Wandered about until at last o'erpowered
By cold and misery, sank into a drift:
And being weary fell into a sleep
To wake no more on earth, and so he died.
And round him lightly fell the fleecy drifts
Forming a shroud of spotless purity.
And there he calmly lay—as beautiful

As when he left our fireside long ago—
For death that changes all had swept aside
The changes of the passing years, and brought
Our wanderer back the boy that went away.

  Down on the hillside, where in summer time
The orchard blossoms that is leafless now,
There, where in childhood he had always played,
Rolling beneath the trees, amid the fruit,
Tossing the golden apples here and there
In sportive mischief, there we carried him,
And laid him gently in a narrow grave
Dug in the stony earth at Christmas-tide.
There can the farmer see the new formed drift
That heaps above it, as he sits all day
Before the window facing toward the slope.
And all day long he sits and watches there,
And rarely speaks, but oft his lips will move
And shape themselves into the name
          of Gabriel.

WILLIAM ALLEN WHITE.

A WILLER CRICK INCIDENT.

Long ago before the 'hoppers an' the drouth of
    semty-four,
Long before we talked of boomin,' long before
    the first Grange store.
Long before they was a city on the banks of
    Willer Crick,
Come a woman doin' washin' an' a little boy
    named Dick :
        Kinder weakly like an' sick ;
        Wasn't even common quick ;
An' the folks said 'at his daddy used to be a
    loonytic.

He was undersized an' ugly an' was tongue-tied
    in his talk ;
He was awkward an' near sighted an' he couldn't
    more'n walk ;
An' the other boys all teased him ; no one knowed
    the reason why,
'Cept to hear his mother pet him : "there, ma's
    angul, there, don' cry."
        When they was nobody nigh
        She would set by him an' sigh ;
An' she'd comb his hair an' kiss him : "Ma's boy
    'ull be well, bye'm bye."

But instead of gettin' stronger Dick grew thin-
    ner ev'ry year ;
An' although his legs got longer, his pore brain
    ketched in the gear.
But he always loved the crick so, an' 'twas there
    'at he 'u'd play ;
Killin' lucky bugs an' buildin' dams 'at always
    broke away.
        But his mother used to pray ;
        "God make Dickie strong, some day"
God 'u'd make him strong an' happy, her "pore
    angul" she 'u'd say.

They was not a long percession when he died,
    an' all I mind
Was a little green farm wagon with two churs
    set in behind.
But it held a lonely mother sobbin' wildly for
    her own ;
An' the sorrow et in deeper for she knew she
    greived alone.
       Mid the sunflow'rs lightly blown.
       Where the sticker weeds are sown,
No one knows the hopes an' heart-aches buried
    'neath that rough-cut stone.

A LITTLE DREAM-BOY.

LITTLE Boy Blue come blow your horn,
And wake up a little man lying forlorn,
Asleep where his life wanders out of the morn.

Little Boy Blue blow a merry, sweet note,
Over the pool where the white lilies float—
Fill out the sails of a little toy boat.

Blow on my dream of a little boy there,—
Blow thro' his little bark-whistle, and snare
Your breath in a tangle of curly brown hair.

Blow and O blow from your fairy land far,
Blow while my little boy wears a tin star,
And rides a stick-horse to a little boy's war.

Blow for the brave man my dream-boy would be,
Blow back his tears when he wakes up to see
His knight errant gone and instead—only me.

Little Boy Blue come blow your horn,
Blow for a little boy lying forlorn,
Asleep where his life wanders out of the morn.

SOME SECULAR QUERIES.

ᴛ the corner of my street,
    There is one
Whom I almost daily meet—
    She's a nun.
And for many a long day
I have wanted nerve to say,
"May I walk along your way,
    Little nun?

"With you I'd be glad to chat,
    Little nun,
'Bout the weather and all that—
    Just for fun.
And, should you remove your mask,
I'd be pretty sure to ask
How you like your lonely task,
    Little nun.

"I am curious to know,
    Little nun,
What you think about the row
    You've begun.
Do you ever sit and muse
On the earthly joys you lose?
Do you ever have the blues,
    Little nun?

"I suspect that you are human,
    Little nun;
And my guess is, that, as woman,
    You've been won.
Does he ever haunt your dreams,
Till his old-time shadow seems
Near you in the noonday beams,
    Little nun?

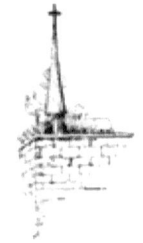

"And you love him anyhow,
    Little nun?
Come, be honest with me now,
    We've begun.
Don't you tell me you have not
An unconsecrated spot—
Do not say you have forgot,
    Little nun.

"For the Lord who made your mother,
      Little nun,
Uses one plan and no other
      To work on.
In the corner where you keep
Woman's fancies, don't you peep
When you think the Lord's asleep,
      Little nun ?"

THE GRADGERRATUN' O' JOE.

WAY down crost the medder an' cow lot,
    Thro' paths made by cattle an' sheep,
Where, cooled in the shade by the tall ellums
        made,
    The old crick has curled up to sleep ;
Down there where the wind sighun' mingles
    'Ith prattelun' waters at play,
An' the coo coo coo of the turtle dove too,
    Seeps in from the dim far away ;
Down there by the banks of the Willer—
    In spring where the sweet-williams grow—
'Twas at this place 'at he, all the time use to be :
    The home of our little boy Joe.
        My Oh—
            How long ago.

Nope ; none a' you couldn't 'a' know'd him,
    Way back there in seventy-four,
When Idy an' me concluded 'at we
    U'd edjicate Joe, rich or pore.
I mind how we skimped, scraped an' worried,
    An' how our first Christmas was dim,
An' how mother cried when we had to decide,
    We couldn't send nothun' to him.
An' nobody else dreams the sorrow,
    'At Idy an' me'd undergo,
A livun' that way all alone ever' day
    A yearnun' an' longun' fer Joe.
            High O
                Long ago.

So Idy an' me went together,
    To hear little Joe gradgerrate ;
Little Joe did I say ? meant big, anyway ;
    He spoke on the subject of "Fate."
An' "my, but the effort was splendid."
    The folks said 'at set by my side,
But I never hyurd a sentence er word—
    An' mother jest broke down an' cried.
I hadn't the heart fer to ask her
    What was the matter, you know ;

Fer I felt she'd a' said ; "Our baby is dead,
   I want back my own little Joe :
         Our Joe
            Of long ago."

So foller me down thro' the cow lot—
   Thro' paths worn by cattle an' sheep,
To where in the shade, by the tall ellums made,
   The old crick is tucked in to sleep ;
Where sighs of the tired breeze whisper
   To quiet the waters at play ;
An' the dreamy coo coo of the turtle dove true,
   Frightens care phantoms away ;
Fer I like to set hyur a thinkun',
   An' astun' the waters 'at flow,
What's come o' the dear little boy 'at played here
   In the days o' the long ago ?
         Our Joe ;
            High ho.

THAT YE BE NOT JUDGED.

From a till the gold coin vanished ;
  It was stolen ; and to-day
From the world the thief is banished—
  Thief's an ugly word to say.
You who never knew of sinning—
  Strong in manhood from your youth :
You who from your life's beginning,
  Never loosened hands with truth—
        Are you the judge?

Yonder walks an erring woman—
  Heartless, hopeless, in the mire ;
Painted, brazen, scarcely human
  In her gaudy trade attire.
Passing her, you give no token—
  You of sinless, baby face—

You, to whom mere words unspoken
   Are the chains of her disgrace—
         Are you the judge?

He was "murdered," said the jury:
   In the viscid, musty cell
Paces one whose fatal fury
   Did the deed; you said: "'Tis well"—
You who take life school-girl fashion,
   You who never spat at Fate—
You who never fondled Passion—
   You who never suckled Hate—
         Are you the judge?

They have broken vows like basting;
   They are underneath the ban;
She, her wifehood's portion wasting—
   He, his world-chance as a man.
You whose heart has ne'er caught anchor
   Deeper than Life's drifting mold;
You who never felt the rancor
   Of a duty-love grown cold—
         Are you the judge?

A RHYME
OF THE DREAM-
MAKER
MAN.

Down near the end of a wander-
ing lane,
That runs 'round the cares of the
day,
Where Conscience and Memory meet
and explain
Their quaint little quarrels away,
A misty air-castle sits back in the dusk
Where brownies and hobgoblins
dwell,
And this is the home
Of a busy old gnome

Who is making up dream-things to sell,
　　　　My dear,
The daintiest dreams to sell.

He makes golden dreams out of wicked men's
　　　sighs.
　He weaves on the thread of a hope
The airiest fancy of pretty brown eyes,
　And patterns his work with a trope.
The breath of a rose and the blush of a wish
　Boiled down to the ghost of a bliss,
　　　　He wraps in a smile
　·　　　Every once in a while,
And calls it the dream of a kiss,
　　　　Dear heart,
　The dream of an unborn kiss.

Last night when I walked through the portals of
　　　sleep
　And came to the weird little den,
I looked in the place where the elf-man should
　　　keep
　A dream that I buy now and then.
'Tis only the sweet happy dream of a day—
　Yet one that I wish may come true—

But I learned from the elf
That you'd been there yourself,
And he'd given my dear dream to you,
Sweetheart,
He'd given our dream to you.

WHERE "A LOVELY TIME WAS HAD."

BILL HUCKS, the item-chaser on the Willer Crick
  Gayzette,
Was the likeliestest hustler that old man McCray
  could get.
As a writer up of runaways, an' funerals, an' shows,
Bill never had an equal nor a rival, goodness
  knows.
So we sent him up a *in*vite to a doins Susie give,
And he writ a piece about it that was fine, as
  sure's you live.
But all I kin remember is, "We hardly need to
  add,
The guests agreed at leaving that a lovely time
  was had."

Oh, yes—now come to think of it—her maw
    cooked up some cake

And pies and floatin' island truck that Susie
    helped to make,

And they was pickle-lilly, too, and beets and jell
    and jam,

And slaw, and chicken-salad, and some sam-
    wiches of ham.

And them Bill said was "viands," which, in writ-
    in' up, he owned,

"Made a tempting feast of good things, and the
    table fairly groaned.

And when the wee sma' hours were come, we
    hardly need to add,

The guests agreed at leaving that a lovely time
    was had."

Old Bill has gone from Willer Crick ; the *Gaz-*
    zette is no more,

For Old McCray has stole away to find the Gold-
    en Shore.

And Susie has been married off for lo! these
    many years,

And some of them that come that night have
    quit this vale of tears ;

But maw has in her scrapbook—'long with little
    Laury's death,
And the pome about the baby and the accident
    to Seth—
The piece about the doins, and to-day it makes
    us glad
To read at Susie's party "that a lovely time was
    had."

JES' LIKE HIM.

Once a man named Jimmy Sellers
  Lived on Willer crick ;
An' fer all yer funny fellers,
  He jes' took the trick.
Kep' a rester'nt where the Hewins
  Boardin' house now is ;
An' at ev'ry show er doin's,
  Seller's geenyus riz :
Blacked up onct an played the nigger ;
  'Nother time the star,—
Some they lowed he was a bigger
  Man 'en Booth by far.
So we never was exactun'—
  Let Jim have his way ;
At his cuttun' up an' actun'
  Folks 'u'd only say :
    " Jes' like him,
      That dag on Jim."

Used to set an' play the *gi*tar
  Shady afternoons,
Till the strings 'u'd fairly glitter
  With his witchy tunes.
I kin almost see him playun'
  Ol' Seebastypool :
Both eyes shet an' him a swayun'
  Like a gash ding fool.
Y' orto hyurd him sing "Lorena"
  Er "Sweet Belle Mahome ;"
I tell you I never seen a
  Feller 'at could come
Nearder to a angel singun'
  'En Jim Sellers could ;
Ef yer eyes 'u'd not be ringun'
  Wet, yer feeluns' would—
      Jes' like Jim—
        Dag on him.

One time when a show was playun'
  In the court-house hall,
Jim he set there without sayun'
  Anything at all.
When 'twas done one of them wimmun
  Met Jim on the street ;

An' we hyrud him plead with brimmun'
  Eyes ; hyrud him entreat
Her to come back ; hyrud him tell her
  How they'd both ferget ;
An' I never seen a feller
  Seem so grieved, an' yet,
When we'd ever cod or joke him
  Jim 'u'd laff an' say,
In a voice 'at 'most 'u'd choke him :
" I was drunk that day"
  Jes' like him—
    That dag on Jim.

TO CHLOE AT SPRINGTIDE.

Now is the day approaching that the poet longs
    to see ;
When "sunny hours" with "greenwood bowers"
    and "fragrant flowers" there be ;
When rhymes come at his bidding, without using
    "know" or "too,"
When "lowing herds" and "loving words" and
    "cooing birds" are due.
When "woods are sweet with perfume," when
    "the languid breezes sigh,"
When "bonny lass" and "waving grass" and
    "sheeny bass" are nigh.
This is the poet's season and the climax doth ap-
    pear,
When Chloe reads her essay to "kind friends
    and teachers dear."

Yon lutist plinks the praises of the maidens as
      they come ;

"To Duty" and "To Beauty" with her tutti
      frutti gum.

This lyrist times his meter "to the sorceress
      whose art"

With "her passion," "tiger fashion" claws a
      gash in Hero's heart.

There are those who sing of Psyche and her mild
      peculiar grace—

In that flighty Grecian nighty, with that highty
      tighty face.

But I'm still true to Chloe in her graduating
      gear—

Who flushes o'er the footlights with "kind friends
      and teachers dear."

Long years ago I loved her and she told me "I
      love you ;"

With the fleetest and completest, sweetest kiss I
      ever knew ;

The mem'ry of that tender look in those coy
      hazel eyes,

When she'd spoken, is a token of my broken
      paradise.

A man is given one such chance to mingle with
the gods ;
If he takes it not, but shakes it, then he makes
it with the clods.
And so I twang a cheerful lyre, and dry the trembling tear,
And bet on other Chloes with "kind friends and
teachers dear."

THE MUSIC WHICH "HATH CHARMS."

"Such songs have power to quiet,
The restless pulse of care."

BEFORE we moved from Willer Crick our Idy used
    to play,
Her organ in the sittun room thro' all the live-
    long day.
The pieces that she liked the most was "Trippun
    Thro' the Dells,"
An' "Siegel's March," an' "Shepherd Boy," an'
    "Monastery Bells."
She knowed the "Cornflow'r Waltz" without a-
    lookun at a note.
An' sang "When You and I Were Young" out of
    her head by rote.
Her pieces long ago had tears, an' tunes a man
    could hum,

But her piany music now goes frizzle, whizzle,
    bum !
T'was writ by furrin labor either "ustski," "off"
    or "iski,"
An' a man—I think she calls him Glazowhiski.

She used to play the second—made it up y' un-
    derstand—
While I sawed on the fiddle "Ol' Zip Coon" or
    Bulyland."
We used to have a medley-piece that give her ma
    a pain,
Of "Devil's Hornpipe," "Martin's Hymn" and
    "Whoop Up Lizy Jane ;"
An' me an' Ide 'u'd play it jest to hyur ma grunt
    around,
'N'en change to "Annie Laurie," till we'd hyur
    a snuffin sound ;
An' n'en we knowed 'at ma fergot, an' banished
    every care—
But law ! them days is over—you jest mighty
    right they air ;
Now when her daddy asts about some piece she
    plays so frisky—
It's "Why, pa, that's a thing from Glazowhiski."

That Glazowhiski feller—or whatever is his
   name—

Has broke into the temple where they keep the
   thing called fame ;

Him an' the man called Motzart, an' Baytoven,
   an' Goono,

An' maybe half a dozen more that Idy raves on so.

But I'm still fer "Lorena" or "They'll Be One
   Vacant Chair"—

The songs that cuddle up an' kiss dry lips of
   mem'ries fair,

An' make 'em smile again ; but then—each feller
   to his taste,

S'I ef them haint dimons then I hanker after
   paste.

But Idy she's fergot 'em—ef I call for one it's
   risky—

It's "Listen to this thing from Glazowhiski."

A PRINT SHOP INCIDENT.

An old typographical error—
One of the old-fashioned school—
    With the old-fashioned stagger,
    The stoop-shouldered swagger,
Sat there on the rickety stool.
He'd "hoofed it clean in from Salina,"
He said, with a make-believe cheer;
    But there rasped in his throat
    A corn-husky note,
  'Twas truly pathetic to hear.

So over we went to the Red-Light
To let the Rum Fiend do its worst;
    For an image of wood
    Most assuredly could
Not withstand such an eloquent thirst.

Some wandering Corsican minstrels
By the door played their plankety plinks;
    He heeded them not,
    But sped to the spot
  Where Cholly was doling the drinks.

Perhaps you have seen an ecstatic
Delirious bliss in the face
    Of a man who's in love,
    As he prances above
The low earthy joys of his race;
Perhaps you've seen pictures of halos
O'er transported features of saints;
    Or looked when she smiled
    In her sleep at a child
  For whom heaven's own artist paints.

Well, if you've seen such an expression
You've an idea then, like as not,
    How his face lighted up
    As he dropped the tin cup
When the liquor got down to the spot.
He rolled his eyes wistfully doorward;
With his hand wiped the liquor away,
    And said in a low,

Quiet voice : " Let us go
Out an' hear them 'ere eyetalics play."

The standard of morals was low then,
Before the descent of St. John ;
     And a man got his rank
     From the size of his tank,
And the number of drinks he had on.
And so when I dream of a heaven,
I think of a place where they say :
     " That's the stuff ; ain't it though ?
     Now come on an' le's go
Out an' hear them dang eyetalics play."

•

SOME SHOP TALK.

WHEN the office is deserted in the evening, and
    your cares
Have trooped off with the devil as he shuffles
    down the stairs,
When you pace about your kingdom like a chain-
    ed and restless pup,
And walk back to view the galley rack to see how
    much is up—
Before you go to supper, put your tired brain to
    soak,
And try to wash the kinks out with a quiet little
    smoke.
      For it's smoke, smoke, smoke,
      Makes the world seem like a joke ;
        With its whirling,
          Curling,
            Swirling,

Where there's nothing that is sterling,
After all its strange unfurling
    Only smoke,
    Purling smoke.

Sit and laugh at "Old Subscriber" and the pa-
    pers marked " refused."
Take a puff at the Alliance that imagines it's
    abused.
Smile in triumph at your banker and the man who
    holds your note ;
O'er your master, that old " plaster," gloat a tran-
    quil, haughty gloat.
And as evening shadows thicken pull your weed
    until it beams ;
Suck sweet sunshine out of sadness in a cloud
    of silver dreams.
    Oh, it's dreams, dreams, dreams ;
    Life is only what it seems ;
      And like mazy,
        Dim and lazy,
    Shifting cloud-forms wierd and crazy.
    Our distinctions are ; so hazy,
      Motes and beams—
      Only dreams.

KING'S EX.

"When the wood is brought in an' the chores 're
    all done, at the dusk, an' the dyun' day
Kisses the old world a smilin' farewell, ere the
    night has come in to pray,
The children romp out in the sunflower weeds,
    in Simmons's vacant lot,—
Maybe they're playin' at hide-an'-go-seek, er pull-
    away jes' like es not ;
Fer the games 'at they have never change very
    much, ner they never git more complex—
An' I'm glad in my heart 'at the children hold on
    to the old fashioned sayin': 'King's Ex.'

Little boy, as you go crost the breakin' of life,
    when your voice shall grow rougher an' deep :
When the cares of the day make you stumble an'
    trip, an' pile on you when you're asleep ;
When you walk in the path where you ortent to
    step, an' feel yourself goun' to fall ;
When no one's around fer to hold to a bit, an'
    yer own little strength is so small ;
Like a child all alone cryin' out in the night,
    when you've got on yer dark blue specs,
You'll clasp yer hands then, as you cross fingers
    now, an' pray fer a sweet King's Ex.

Little girl, though they call you a tom-boy to-
    day, to-morrow they'll let out your dress ;
An' with every flounce an' each ruffle an' braid, a
    joy an' a care comes, I guess.
Some day in the big unknown future, perhaps,
    you'll taste the vile dregs in the glass
You drank from so wildly an' blindly an' mad.
    your hand could not yield it to pass.
When you feel, in your bitterness, sorrow an'
    shame, the cruel stones thrown at your sex,
When men shall be deaf to your piteous cry—
    ask God for a little King's Ex.

A WAIL IN B MINOR.

Oh ! What has become of the ornery boy,
Who used to chew slip'ry elm, "rosum" and
     wheat ;
And say "jest a coddin " and "what d'ye soy ;"
And wear rolled up trousers all out at the seat.

And where is the boy who had shows in the barn,
And "skinned a cat backards" and turned "sum-
     mersets "
The boy who had faith in a snake-feeder yarn,
And always smoked grape vine and corn ciggar-
     ettes.
Where now is the small boy who spat on his bait,
And proudly stood down near the foot of the
     class,

And always "went barefooted" early and late,
And washed his feet nights on the dew of the
    grass.

Where is the boy who could swim on his back,
And dive and tread water and lay his hair, too ;
The boy who would jump off the spring-board
    kerwhack,
And light on his stomach as I used to do.

O where and O where is the old-fashioned boy?
    Has the old-fashioned boy with his
        old-fashioned ways,
    Been crowded aside by the Lord
        Fauntleroy,
    The cheap polished bric-a-brac full
        of alloy,
    Without the pure gold of the rolick-
        ing joy
      Of the old-fashioned boy in the
        old-fashioned days?

A GROUP OF HUMBLE CRADLE SONGS.

A WILLER CRICK LULLABYE.

O LISSUN an' hush-a-bye, while daddy sings,
    Bylo, pa's littul man, do ;
An' ma reds the table an' clears up the things,
    Bylo, pa's littul man, do.
I'll make up a song fer you out of my head,
About all the fairies what's livun er dead ;
An' if you go bylo, I'll bet 'tull come true,
    Bylo, pa's littul man, do.

Two littul boys onct went to bed in a loft,
    Bylo, pa's little man, do ;
An' both of 'em heerd purty music as soft,
    As Bylo, pa's littul man, do ;
So one littul shaver jest shut his eyes tight,

An' played with the fairies the hull live-long
     night,—
The other'n who wouldn't heerd booggers go
     "boo!"
    Bylo, pa's littul man, do.

So run littul tyke with the fairies an' play,
    Bylo, pa's littul man, do—
Wood-tag, er bean-bag, er ol' pull-away,—
    Bylo, pa's littul man, do.
They'll take you way up to a world above this,
An' let you slide down on the thread of a kiss,
With ma at the bottom a wakun' up you—
    Bylo, pa's littul man, do.

A JIM STREET LULLABYE.

Hursh-a-bye, sweetheart,
    O, hursh an' láy still,
Mommer 'ull stay with you,
    Dear, come w'ot will;
Mommer c'u'd not live without you—my pet—
Mommer is proud of you—she don' regret;
Gawd! how can some people want to ferget;
    Hursh-a-bye, sweet, and lay still—dear.

Hursh a-bye, sweet-heart,
    O hursh an' lay still ;
Lookie at them purties
    There on the sill !
Dearie, them's posies, an' some day we'll go,
Back to the ol' place whur wild posies grow—
Jest us alone—whur they'll nobody know—
    Hursh a-bye, sweet, an' lay still—dear.

Hursh a-bye sweet-heart,
    O hursh, an' lay still ;
Purtiest dreams
    May your littul heart fill.
W'y shouldn't they, like es not ? and come true ?
You hain't done nothin' rich babies don' do :
Me an' the angels an Jesus loves you !
    Hursh a-bye, sweet, an' lay still--dear.

SISTER MARY'S LULLABYE.

Zhere, zhere, 'ittul b'o', sistuh 'll wock you to
    s'eep,
  Hush-a-bye O, darlene, wock-a-bye, b'o',
An' tell you the stowy about the b'ack sheep—
  Wock-a-bye my 'ittul b'over.

A boy onct said "b'ack sheep, you dot any wool?"
"Uh-huhm" said the lambie, "I dot free bags
    full."
An' where Murry went w'y the lamb's sure to doe,.
They's mowe of zis stowy—I dess I don' know ;
  But hush-a-bye O, darlene, wock-a-bye b'o',
    Wock-a-bye my 'ittul b'over.

O, mama says buddy tomed stwaight down f'om
    Dod ;
  Hush-a-bye O, uh-huhm, wock-a-bye b'o',
'At doctuh mans bwunged him, now isn't zhat
    odd—
  Wock-a-bye my 'ittul b'over.
For papa says, "doctuhs is thiefs so zhey be."
An' thiefs tain't det up into Heaven you see !
I dess w'en one do's up an' dets sent below,
He's dot to bwing wif him a baby or so ;
  Hush-a-bye O, uh-huhm, wock-a-bye b'o'.
    Wock-a-bye, my 'ittul b'over.

But sistuh loves b'o' anyhow if he's dood,
  Hush-a-bye O, sweetie, wock-a-bye b'o',
Better'n tandy er infalid's food—
  Wock-a-bye sistuh's own b'over.

An' some day when buddy drows up to a man,
W'y sistuh an' him 'ull 'ist harness ol' Fan,
An' dwive off to Heaven the fuist zhing you know,
An' bwing ever' baby back what wants to doe.
    Zhen hush-a-bye O, sweetie, wock-a-bye b'o',
      Wock-a-bye sistuh's own b'over.

THEIR POOR DADDY.

If daddy had plenty of money, my dear,
  My ! what a good daddy he'd be.
He'd buy ev'rything in the world purty near
  To give sister Murry and me.
He'd git us the crick fer to wade in, 'y jings,
And down by the ford where it ripples and sings,
He'd strain out the sunshine and song, and make
     things
  To play with, fer Murry and me.
  —My, what a good daddy he'd be,
    And he'd buy us the trees
    If Murry would tease—
If daddy had plenty of money.

If daddy had plenty of money, I bet,
  He'd be the best daddy on earth.

They wouldn't be anything we couldn't get,
  No matter how much it was worth.
To play circus under he'd git us the sky,—
To make beads fer Murry, the stars upon high,—
To have pillow fights with, the clouds that blow
      by,—
  No matter how much they was worth—
  He'd be the best daddy on earth.
    Why he'd buy us the moon
    Fer a toy balloon—
If daddy had plenty of money.

If daddy hain't got any money, I guess,
  He wouldn't sell Murry and me.
We're tow-headed skeezickses, that's what he
      says,
  And scalawags, that's what we be.
An' n'en when the Riddles ride by in their rig
'Ithout any children, ol' daddy feels big,
And tells ma he won't fer a farm and a pig
  Swap off sister Murry and me—
  We're skeezickses, that's what we be.
    But Murry, and me
    Are his fortune, says he—
If daddy hain't got any money.

A RICKETY RHYME OF YE OLDEN TIME.

Whylom ther ben a witteless Curl,
   He wont in Olden Tymes ;
And eke ther ben a Giddie Girl,
   And he at hire hys Heort did hurl,
As Wyghtes have done thro alle the Worl',
   So tellen Olden Rhymes.

Sche grette thys Curl with doun-cast eyes,
   Lik Maydes of Olden Tymes ;
I nolde say whens sche get Hire Syghes,
   Nor gif sche seemed hire Glad Surprise :
No boke canne say whenne woman lyes—
   Not even Olden Rhymes.

He tok thys Sweteheort to ye Schowe—
  Ye Pley of Olden Tymes ;
They sate hem in ye Choyseste Rowe
  For he hys super wolde forgoe
That he at Nyght myght seme to throw
  On Dogge ; so say ye Rhymes.

But whenne Trewe Love thys Curl did make—
  Thys Curl of Olden Tymes—
Sche lysten softly whyl he spake,
(I gesse sche wot hys Purs ben brake),
Fr O ! sche gave him an Hard Schake,
  So tellen Olden Rhymes.

So full of Sorewe ben hys Cuppe—
  Thys Curl of Olden Tymes—
He tramp-ed alle ye Dayseys uppe
Benethe hire Casement, and ye Puppe
Coude not hys Serenayding stoppe ;
  He made thes Cadent Rhymes :

"You came dere, last Nyght in a Raydiaunt
    Dreme'
  And ye Day yt ys ful of your Perfume yet—
—Fragraunt with you, and so Swete doth yt seme,

That God moste have sprinkled from yesterday's
     Streme,
  (Where our Lyves ran together unchoked by
     Regret),
A Chalyce of Water that lay in ye Gleme
Of your eyes o'er my Heort, and a myst from ye
     Dreme
  Fills alle ye Day with your Perfume yet."

Now whenne thys Wyght hys Whyskers grew—
  Thys Wyght of Olden Tyme— ·
He get a Wyf as Wyse Men do,
  And lyed about hys First Love Trewe—
—Which schowes he wot a Thing or Two :
     So tellen Olden Rhymes,
       Betymes,
        So tellen Rymes.

·

THE FORMAL ANNOUNCEMENT.

THAT Mister Sims, who's comed out here
To see our Jen fer 'bout a year,
W'y yesterday walked in the store
Whur he has never been before.
Yes-*sir* an' you'd ist orto saw
The way he talked polite to pa.
An' 'en they both looked, in the face,
Zif they'd been 'vited to say grace,
'N' druther not ; ist like the mens
We boarded durin' conference.
At last pa ups an' says it was
All right, what ever Jennie does.

That night at supper pa says :   " Jen
I seen that Sims to-day," an' 'en
She doused the lasses on her mush—
Jen did—an' says :   "Now pa, you hush."
An' pa an' ma laffed fit to kill,
An' ast Jen when she thinks she will.
So, when they sent me off to bed,
I heard ol' Mister Simsy said :
" W'y, Jen, you'll break your daddy's chair "
But Jen she whispers " I don' care.
We got another ; but," says she.
" You needn't tell the fambilee."

THE NEW WRINKLE ON MR. BILL.

I LIKE it when they's company
Comes to visit us fer we
Gets to have the goodest things—
Ist like Sunday ; 'n'en 'y jings,
Me an' Wullie gets a chance
To wear our littul boughton pants—
Uncle Hiram give us when
He was here onct—ist like men.

Pa says, Wullie he's so dumb
Bout behavin', he can't come
To the table any more :
Cause ma most went th'ue the floor,
Th'other day, when Mrs. Gus
Vandegrif she et with us.
When we all got done with soup,
Wullie he sets up a hoop :
" Ma ! come take my bowl away !
What 'you wunged that bell fer ?   Ay ?"

MR. BILL'S INSOMNIA.

LITTUL Wullie—he's my brother—
    He hain't got a lick a sense.
Pa says Wullie's like his mother—
    He is ist so very dense.
Th' other mornin Wullie's piller-
    Case it had some holes in it ;
An' we thought 'at ma 'u'd kill 'er
    Self a laffin fore she quit.
Pa, he says "Geemy-my, Jenny,
    Tell us what you're laffin 'bout."
Ma says "Wullie can't sleep any
    Cause he says his dreams leak out."

"BUD" AND THE HATCHET MYTH.

ONCT was a boy an' he couldn't lie ;
No sir, no matter how he try.
N'en his dad w'y he up an' said :
"George git the wood 'fore you go to bed."
George didn't like it a bit 'adburn,
T' bring in the wood when it wasn't his turn ;
But allee samee he mosied out,
Picked up his ax, an' he looked about
Wher was a churry tree 'at his dad
Bragged on what fine churries it had.
N'en w'y George lit in an' chopped
Th'ol' tree down an' never stopped
Till he cut it into sticks so small,
Piled way up ginst the kitchen wall.

Well purty soon his dad comed in,
Looked at the wood, an' said 'with a grin :
"George, who got all this nice wood ?"
George didn't lie cause he never could—
But telled his dad jest the hones' fac's :
" I done it sir, with my littul ax."

FATHER'S LITTLE JOKE.

FATHER used to rig the girls about us bein' pore,
An' go on lots about things what's a go'n' to hap-
     pen shore :
The hot winds an' the hoppers an' the chinch-
     bugs in the wheat,
An' holler-horn an' ten cent corn ;—you never
     seen the beat
Of how he used to grunt around—jest gasin' like
     you see—
"We 're goin' to the pore-house Sue, lickety-
     split,'' sezee.
Then, snappin' of his galluses an' backin' to the
     fire,
He 'd stretch an' smile a little while and puff
     his reekin' briar ;

An' takin' in the sittun room from every which-
    a-way,
"This is good enough fer pore folks," is what
    father 'd always say.

F'rinstunce say some Sunday when the Rug-
    gleses drove down ;—
Unload a hull dern wagon full; jes' like a small
    sized town ;
An' father 'd look at mother an' he 'd ast her ef
    she 's got
That johnny-cake and side of bacon left—es like
    es not.
Then mother 'd tie her apern on an' guess that
    she 'd make out :—
(T'u'd do you good ef you jest could see mother
    flax about.)
Well—they 'd be mashed potatoes, chicken,
    turnips, squash an' slaw,
Tomato stew an' string-beans too, perserves an'
    pie an'—law,
Dead oodles of brown gravy; an' nen—after
    father 'd pray—
"This is good enough fer pore folks," is what
    father 'd always say.

The night Jane come home cryin', when they give
  her her divorce,

The girls an' me an' mother we made over her
  a-course ;

But father stayed around the barn an' mother
  passed the plates,

When supper come an' made up somethin' 'bout
  his fixin' gates.

Then after supper father came an' set around an'
  smoked,

An' looked at Jane time an' again, 'zif he 'd a-like
  to joked

An' churped her up, but dassent 'n' yet wanted
  her to know

How glad he was she 'd come to us, but could
  n't jest say so.

At bed time father pinched Jane's cheeks—his
  dear old fashioned way—

" Home's good enough fer pore folks," was all
  father's voice could say.

THE MAIDEN AND THE PRINCE.

THERE 's a half-forgotten story or the echo of a
    song,
That is tangled in the meshes of my mem'ry, and
    a throng
Of knights in jeweled armor pass in dignified
    parade,
Across my fitful fancy, while, upon a palisade,
A wraith of regal radiance, illumes the legend
    fair :
Of the maid behind the trellis and the prince
    who kissed her hair.

There's a glitter and a glamour in the telling of
    the tale,

And a golden thread of love is wrapt around the
    rugged mail,
Till its silky strands seem stronger than the woof
    of love we know,
As it shimmers in the sunshine on the hills of
    long ago.
And so lovers of these latter days look back with
    mute dispair
At the maid behind the trellis and the prince
    who kissed her hair.

Yet the lily lady's lover was a roisterer who
    fought
Many brutal bloody battles for the booty that
    they brought ;
And his heart benumbed and callous, seared with
    passion could not feel
The perfumed breath of Love through Hope's
    enchanted chambers steal.
'Twas the halo of some poet's love that lit the
    fabled pair :
The maid behind the trellis, and the prince who
    who kissed her hair.

HOW IT HAPPENED.

WHEN God was aglow with His work on the
     world,
  That stood on the structure of Faith,
He hewed out the Winter and lustily whirled
His hammer aloft, and with fancy unfurled
He dreamed out the Summer ; then as His lips
     curled
  In a smile (like a Heavenly wraith,)
His hands slowly fashioned the smile of His face,
  And wrought there the beautious thing
Unknown to the Worker who bent o'er the place
Where Winter should be—full of joy at the grace
Of His dream ; but at last, God beholding the
     trace
  Of His smile on the world—called it Spring.

WOMANHOOD.

I KISSED her baby, and its hazel eyes
   Beamed through my soul, where, in a dim re-
      cess,
   There is a pictured face on which distress
Plays hide and seek with hope; a tear-drop dries,
Warmed by her parting smile; again she tries
   To reach me with a zephyr-blown caress.
   This, I in anguish had called " Faithlessness "
And pricked it on my heart with poisoned dyes.

The baby's lips were sweet with drowsy wine
   Pressed out of dreams, by fragrant mem'ry
      stirred.
   I drank my fill and yielded to its mood.
And when I woke the picture still was mine;
   (By baby lips the title had been blurred,)
      And underneath was written, " Womanhood."

.

"COMFORT SCORNED OF DEVILS."

O LET me keep the sorrow in my heart,
   That God has sent, nor hope that it may go ;
   O rather let me pray I may not know
The empty day when sorrow shall depart,
And leave me callous with no tears to start,
   When mem'ry trips upon my heart-strings,
      though
   My soul shall writhe with anguish,—be it so :
Why, only quick hearts quiver neath a dart !

For Joy or Love or Sorrow keeps the heart alive,
   And moistens it with Hope, that parching heat
     Of passion may not crust it as a glove.
Then let me live, O God, and ever strive
   To hallow Sorrow ; O it is as sweet
     To live for Sorrow as to live for Love.

AFTER WHILE.

There was a day when anguish gashed my heart,
  And fevered grief throbbed through my fren-
    zied brain,
  And beat upon my soul a rhythmed strain,
That echoed in the songs that used to start
Whene'er I touched the lute-strings of my art.
  O, sad sweet songs that sorrow keyed to pain,
  And timed to dripping heart-blood and the
    rain
  Of unshed tears, that you and I should part!

That day is gone; I cannot strike the chords
  That sobbed of woe they vainly would con-
    ceal;
    Nor does my numbed heart quiver neath its
      thongs.
To-day dry eyes scan only empty words,
  A soul balmed in content can scarcely feel;
    Since comfort stemmed my wounds and still-
      ed the songs.

A VALENTINE.

In those old days, the days now dead and sleeping,
In those old days the dream-world still is keeping,
In those old days, the days of young life's gladness,
In those old days so full of first love's madness,
In those old days—you recollect them do you?—
In those old days I sang this love song to you :

The wind and the world may be cold to you dear,
  Ho bonnie maiden with eyes so blue,
For winds are as cruel as worlds are drear,
Then come to me darling with never a fear,
Come, come, come, sweetheart, come to me here,
  Ho bonnie cling to your true love.

And yet to-day heart throbs to heart no greeting ;
And yet to-day we only bow at meeting ;
And yet to-day in two graves love is moulding,
And yet to-day one past two hearts are holding ;
And yet to-day by all the past worth living ;
And yet O friend ! hear me and be forgiving.

South wind !
Soft wind !
Kiss the hills again,
Start the rills again,
Soft wind !
South wind !
Kiss and wake the sleeping spring,
Till she pulses everything.
As when autumn's here,
And the woods are sere
And the passion of the summer's gone,
Do the pensive days,
Filled with April haze
Seem to turn the year back to its dawn,
So my friend may we
Strangers though we be—
Now that all love's fires are drenched for aye,
Kindly spring recall,
And be friends far all—
Friends through all the Indian summer day.
Soft wind !
South wind !
Kiss the hills again,
Wake the spring and then
Waft the thorns and ashes all away.

A SONG FOR MISTRESS SYLVIA.

Who is Sylvia? What is she,
That all our swains commend her ?—*Two Gentlemen of Verona*

I fain would sing to Sylvia a halting rhyme or two,
  With a high ho lawsy daisy, high ho hum,
For other bards have sung her praises since the
      lyre was new,
    Singing hey and lack-a-day until the bright
      days come.
And when he sings to Sylvia, each singer whis-
      pers low,
A name he dare not weave into his melody, and so,
Fair Sylvia has charms from all the goddesses ago.
    Sing a hey and lack-a-daisy with a high ho hum.

O every song to Sylvia by lover ever writ,
  With a high ho lawsy daisy, high ho hum.
Is sweeter far than silence though it jars a little
      bit,

Singing hey and lack-a-day until the bright
days come.
For having loved and told of it, and having tried
to sing,
What matters if the trembling note hath not a
golden ring ;
O joy hath breathed on some lorn heart to move
that rusty string,
With its hey and lack-a-daisy and its high ho
hum.

So I fain would sing to Sylvia a halting rhyme or
two,
With a high ho dearie, dearie high ho hum,
A-sighing words to Sylvia my heart would say to
you,
Singing hey and lack-a-day until the bright
days come.
This song is made for you, my love, whose name
is whispered low,
This heart and voice are trembling as this husky
tune doth flow ;
And her who knows she's Sylvia—this world may
never know,
Singing hey ho dearie, dearie high ho hum.

.

THE EXODUS OF ELDER TWIGGS.

I BEEN here in the city now since last Thanks-
    giving day,

A-savin' steps for Nelly—chorin' like as you
    might say ;

A-dubbin' 'round fer David and a putterin' about,

A-takin' care of little Bill when him an' her goes
    out.

A-course I've hed my pastimes an' the things
    that I admire,

Like watchin' people movin' safes an' runnin' to
    a fire,

An' talkin' to the milkman—singin' " Buckle Up
    My Shoe "

Fer little Bill to laff at like his mother used to do.

But 'en my other daughter's writ fer me to come
        agin—
So I guess I'll go to Julia when the spring sets in.

They hain't no settled weather much till after
        March I know ;
I want to be on deck, though, as the sayin' used
        to go.
I want to be on hand the day the younguns rake
        the yard,
An' the night they have thur bonfire ; an' when
        Julia rends her lard
I want to cut the fat fer her, an' if they kill a
        shoat,
To get a little fresh spring meat, I want to have
        a vote
In givin' Budd the fixins an' the tail to little Net ;
An' someone's left the stone off of the pickle
        pork I bet.
The brine must need a change by now—to let it
        spoil's a sin—
So I guess I'll go to Julia when the spring sets in.

I want to be around the day they take the peach-
        blows out,

An' he'p Budd sort 'em over an' to find the long-
    est sprout.

I want to scrape a apple jest uncovered from the
    ground

Fer Julia's youngest baby, while the ol' familiar
    sound

Of stirrin' up the buckwheat cakes the hour of
    bed time tells,

An' soothes the heart to rest jes' like a chime of
    home-made bells.

I want to see the children in thur nighties like a
    swarm

Of little home-made angels bring thur pillows
    down to warm.

I want to taste ol' home-made joy and home-made
    love of kin—

So I guess I'll go to Julia when the spring sets in.

I think 'at when the weather limbers up and
    easies down,

I'd like it say some Sunday fer to jes' sneak
    through the town,

An' rack out fer the timber, takin' little Budd
    along

An' him an' me smoke grapevine an' pertend

they's nothin' wrong ;

An' stretch out in the sunshine on the gravel by
    the crick

A-knowin' meetin's goin' on—not carin', though,
    a lick ;

A-gettin' loads of red buds an' sweet-will-yums
    an' (b'gosh)

A mess of greens to boil fer Monday's dinner
    when they wash !

    *   *   *   *   *   *   *

This boughten jam of joy is spread on city life
    too thin ;

So I guess I'll go to Julia when the spring sets in.

TERPSICORE ON WILLER CREEK.

THE daughters of Terpsichore who sit at Pallas'
        feet,
    And overlook the festival of dancing,
In point of style and makeup may be very hard
        to beat—
As supple, soft-eyed houris they're entrancing.
                But a tanned cheeked deity,
                Living in the Used-to-be.
Could beat these maids with cards and spades in
        bloom ;
                For she reigned on Willer Crick,
                And presided fair and chic,
O'er the "rags" we used to give before the boom.

The "rags" we used to give before we platted
    out the place,
  Before we had the opry house to splurge in,
Were free and easy gatherings of home-made
    country grace,
  And everybody came without the urgin';
      Oh, the fiddle and the horn,
      And the organ, wheezed and worn,
Made an itchy, twitchy, music in the gloom
      Of the busy work-aday
      So that sorrow stayed away
From the "rags" we used to give before the boom.

The caller-off and fiddler was a simple home-
    ly soul
  Who had one waltz in all his repertory;
His long suit was his "cowdrills" and the ever-
    flowing bowl,
  And the "Irish Washerwoman" was his glory.
      But he tickled up our heels
      With his old Virginia reels
Like an airy joyful fairy in the room;
      For then none of us were rich,
      Nor were parvynew and sich—
At the "rags" we used to give before the boom.

IF YOU GO AWAY.

ROUNDEL.

IF you go away, a wild Woe will weep o'er the
  place
Where you sit ; she will stretch her stark arms
  out and sobbingly pray
That Death cool the slow-throbbing pain in her
  empty embrace—
   If you go away.

Perhaps it is better to go ere you tire of the play—
Ere the hulls of your hopes are torn open to leave
  bitter trace
Of the worm—when your hopes are first blush-
  ing and ere they decay.

I know it is hard to be still and look Death in
      the face ;

With lips sweet and dewy from Life's morning
      kisses to say :

I am ready.   But God ! 't will be harder to keep
      in the race—

          If you go away.

OUT IN THE DARK.

Dear, I must go.
The old clock says it: nine—ten—hark !
　Of course the old clock can not know,
　That every hour-beat is a blow
　Upon my heart—I love you so.
　Some day we'll taunt the old clock though—
Dear I must go—out in the dark.

　Out in the dark,
Where, on the night wind sweet I throw
　A kiss my love guides to its mark ;
　And where each mellow heav'nly spark
　Joins in a love song that the lark
　Translates at morn ; where dreams embark—
Out in the dark—dear, I must go.

Dear, I must go,
For God hath willed it, loved one, hark !
  And He alone can truly know
  How crushed and bruised beneath His blow
  Our hearts are, for we love love so —
  Some day we'll triumph o'er Death though—
Dear, I must go—out in the dark.

Out in the dark,
Where hov'ring near you I shall throw
  My love about you, and you'll mark
  My presence by the glowing spark
  That mem'ry breathes on ; th' meadow lark—
  At dusk will call *you* to embark—
Out in the dark.　Dear, *I* must go.

L'ENVOI.

Hold to my hand, dear heart, for oh,
  I am so weak, yes, dear, blind—stark :
And God—I do not want to go
  Out in the dark.